Amaricio's Omega

Draco International #1

An MM/MPreg Shifter Romance

I0539763

A.J. Stone

Amaricio's Omega (Draco International 1)
Copyright © July 2018 by A.J. Stone
Print ISBN: 978-1-942414-52-0

Editor: Nicoline Tiernan
Cover Artist: Nicoline Tiernan

Published by Lost Goddess Publishing LLC

About Amaricio's Omega

Amaricio Granger was looking for an assistant, one who would be thoughtful and loyal to the hard-working, alpha dragon shifter. He wanted someone to pick up his dry cleaning and bring coffee. He hadn't been looking for an omega mate.

Edgar Vidal never thought he'd get the job. What did a personal assistant do, anyway? When he showed up for the job interview as the only candidate not wearing a power suit, he knew he didn't have a chance. But that was before a chance encounter with the ruggedly handsome CFO of Draco International.

Finding love was easy, but when the most powerful dragon in the Sharp-Winged Tribe disapproves of the union, staying together may prove impossible. How much is Amaricio willing to sacrifice to be with the omega who won his heart?

Welcome to Draco International, home of high-powered dragon shifters who live by their own rules. This 45,000-word MPreg novel includes passionate and explicit sexual content, as well as some violence. Suitable for adult audiences.

Chapter 1—Edgar

"You'll do fine, Edgar. Don't stress yourself out to the point where you throw up." On the other end of the line, Brielle sighed.

Edgar's younger sister and best friend was his rock and his cheerleader, but at times like this, he wished she wouldn't mention vomiting. It made his stomach churn. "Brielle, don't say the T-U word."

With his phone pressed to his ear, he bolted to the nearest bathroom. Then he rethought that strategy. The last thing he needed was the lobby full of potential candidates for the job and any other staff to hear him retching. He burst out of there and found an out-of-the-way restroom.

"Edgar, don't you dare do it." Brielle spoke firmly. "Breath. Inhale through your nose. Exhale through your mouth. You're good enough. You're smart enough. You earned this interview."

As if she had magic powers, her assurances made the sick feeling go away. "I wish you were hiring me."

"When I'm a famous singer, you can be my assistant, I promise. Hey—why don't you look at this like practice for taking care of me when I become a diva?"

He laughed. Brielle was the farthest thing from a diva he'd ever met. She volunteered every week to lead sing-alongs in retirement homes, and she fostered homeless dogs. If anything, she was too humble. Later that day, she planned to take the dogs she was fostering to an adoption picnic. They'd made special dog treats the night before to mark the occasion.

A notification sounded on his phone. "That's me. It's almost time for my interview. I'm going to wash my hands and get back to the lobby where I'll be lost in a sea of men and women wearing suits and vying for the same job."

"Luck and love," Brielle said, using their shorthand for *Best of luck* and *I love you.* "Call me after."

"Luck and love to you too. I will. Bye."

He slid the phone into his bag, and then he looked around, careful to keep his gaze away from the urinals where several men did their business. The restroom was clean. It had pale tan tile on the walls with ocher accents, and stacks of paper hand towels were near each soap dispenser. The public bathroom in this building was nicer than anyplace he'd ever lived. There was no way he was getting this job.

First off, he didn't have a suit. The nicest interview outfit he'd managed to put together consisted of khaki pants and a white dress shirt. He didn't even own a tie. He looked down at his brown dress shoes. Though they were shiny and well-kept, they'd seen better days. He looked good, but in no way did he look the part of personal assistant to Amaricio Granger, CFO of Draco International.

He wasn't sure what a CFO did or what Draco International sold, but he figured that a personal assistant did things like schedule dentist appointments and walk the dog. He could do that and stay out of the business end of things. Of course, everyone in the lobby waiting for their turn at an interview had a different interpretation of what the job duties meant. In all likelihood, they were right and he was wrong.

With a sigh, he surrendered to the inevitable disappointment. The interview would be good experience for his next one. He'd ask for feedback about what he could do better. People liked to do those types of things.

He used the facilities, and then he washed his hands.

A man came up next to him, talking on the phone in an unfamiliar language. His voice came out in a low rumble that Edgar felt more than heard, and he had a cologne that piqued Edgar's curiosity. Much like the others in the lobby, he wore a suit and tie. He had a rugged face with sharp features and strong lines. His dark hair and eyes added a sort-of mystique that made him handsome instead of unfortunate-looking. He had a distinguished air about him, an authority Edgar would want in a personal assistant. This guy got things done.

He ended the call and dried his hands.

As he turned away, Edgar noticed a crumb on the man's cheek.

"Hey, you have—"

The guy swiveled back, one brow raised.

Edgar lifted a hand to his own cheek to indicate the location of the crumb. "Blueberry crumble?"

He wiped at his cheek, missing the crumb. Instead of using the mirror to check, his gaze concentrated on Edgar. "Better?"

Edgar brushed it away, noting the smoothness of the man's skin. "The bakery down the street has the best blueberry crumble muffins. When I'm being very bad, I get one."

"Bad?" The accompanying frown was downright menacing.

Keeping a friendly smile because he realized the man had misunderstood his intention, he explained. "They have like a thousand calories. I swear, I eat one, and a love handle pops out to wave at me."

The man's sinful gaze wandered up and down Edgar's body, and then he seemed to dismiss it entirely. Okay, maybe the sinful part had been only in Edgar's mind. He sucked on the left side of his lower lip, a nervous habit Brielle said was endearing but probably wasn't all that great. His gaze fell to the man's tie.

It was a power tie, deep red with flecks of gold thread. "Oh, that blueberry sure gets away from you."

The guy's gaze dropped to the tie, and his growl matched his expression.

"I have a stain stick." Edgar opened the leather messenger bag he'd picked up at a charity resale shop for five dollars. A short rummage brought him to his prize. He held it up. "Here."

The frown was gone, but the quizzical look was back.

"It works. I swear. I just used it on my shirt this morning." He untucked a corner where he'd spilled coffee and lifted it to so the rugged man could see. "Coffee stain, gone. It's like magic."

Rugged man took it and dabbed at the stain until it disappeared. Then he handed the stain stick back. "Thanks."

"If this restroom had air dryers, you could dry your tie." He secured the lid on the stain stick and tucked it back into his bag. "Hopefully it'll dry before your interview."

"Interview?"

Edgar held out his hand. "I'm Edgar. Good luck today."

That confused look was back. "You're here to interview for the personal assistant job?" The guy shook his hand, but he made it seem like it was his idea.

The question made him self-conscious. He didn't know anything about the man or the company, and he hadn't thought it was the kind of job that required a suit. "Yeah. Snowball's chance for me, but maybe I'll treat myself to a blueberry crumble after."

The confusion morphed back into a frown. Rugged man came by that face honestly. "Why would you think you don't have a chance?" A gleam in his dark eyes demanded answers, and Edgar found himself giving them.

"No experience, and I don't own a suit. I was thinking this would be the kind of job where I picked up the dry cleaning, walked the dog, and went on coffee runs. Maybe do some emergency grocery shopping. I don't know—stuff a busy guy doesn't have time to do." He motioned in the direction of the lobby and leaned forward. "Those people all have business degrees. I don't know the first thing about business."

"But you're still going through with the interview?"

Edgar shrugged. "It'll be a learning experience."

The light in the man's eyes changed to thoughtful. His gaze wandered up and down Edgar again, this time with an appraising light. "You helped me out even though you think we're competing for the same job."

"It doesn't hurt to be kind, and you're the one who has to live with yourself when you aren't." He tilted his head in a farewell to the strangely handsome stranger, and he returned to the lobby to wait for his interview.

He made it just in time.

A petite woman with black hair tied up in a neat bun commanded the space. "Everyone who has an eight-forty appointment, follow me."

Edgar and nine other people scrambled after her. She led them into a conference room.

"Have a seat."

The crowd scrambled for the seats as if the last one standing was going to be eaten by a shark. One woman even pulled a chair out from under a man. Not one to be pushy, Edgar waited for the others to sort themselves out. They did, and that's when he realized there were nine chairs.

The petite woman crooked a finger at him. He went to the front of the room. "Thank you for coming," she said. "You can go now."

The chair thing had been a test, and he'd failed. Though he'd known the job was a longshot, he still felt a bit of a letdown. He offered his hand. "Thank you, and you have a great day."

Surprise flitted across her features as she shook his hand. Her mouth opened like she was searching for something to say, but the door opened before anything came out.

Rugged man stepped inside. His gaze zeroed in on Edgar, and he pointed. "Him."

The lady with the tight bun seemed to find her voice. "You're sure?"

The frown he directed at her was nothing like the ones Edgar had seen in the restroom. This one answered the lady's question while simultaneously taking her to task for asking it. He left, closing the door behind him.

Edgar made to leave, but she stopped him. "Oh, no. You can't leave now. You got the job."

He motioned to the closed door. "That's what that meant?"

"Yes." Her smile softened. "Congratulations. You're now Mr. Amaricio Granger's personal assistant."

Okay, this was worse. Maybe. He had no fucking clue what a personal assistant did. He'd thought the interview process might clarify it for him, and then the next time he went for a job like this, he'd know what he was up against. In a daze, he followed the woman out of the room and into an elevator.

"I'm Kimbra Braysar, Mr. Granger's office manager." The elevator opened, and she got out. He followed. She power-walked past an administrative assistant's desk and into an office. Three men jumped to their feet. "This is..." She frowned. "What is your name?"

"Edgar Vidal."

"This is Edgar Vidal. He's going to be Mr. Granger's new personal assistant. Give him the necessary paperwork. One of you dismiss the applicants downstairs and in conference room 17-B." She faced Edgar next. "When you're finished here, go to security and get the necessary clearances. Then come up to see me. Mr. Granger will want to go over your duties as soon as possible."

Edgar had not expected to start work this soon. He'd thought the hiring process would take at least a week. "Can I make a phone call?"

With the lift of one brow, Kimbra asked a question. She'd definitely learned that move from Mr. Granger.

"My sister. She's kind of waiting for news one way or the other." He held up his phone. "I'll be quick."

"Send a text. Mr. Granger doesn't like to be kept waiting." With that, Kimbra left the office.

The man at the nearest desk approached holding out a hand. "Hi, Edgar. I'm Vander. Welcome to the Draco International family. I'll help you get your paperwork squared away." He indicated a chair next to his desk for Edgar to sit in. "I have to apologize for not being ready. We thought the interviews were today, so we didn't expect to process anyone until tomorrow at the soonest."

"The interviews were today." Edgar knew how Vander felt. He wasn't sure it was all for real yet. "Mine lasted all of ten seconds, maybe. It was weird."

"Weird?" This question came from the next desk over. "How so?"

Edgar read the man's name badge clipped to his shirt. "Well, Julio, they took ten of us into a room with nine chairs."

"Do you have your resume?" Vander held out a hand. "I'll need your license and social security card as well."

Digging in his messenger bag, he found the requested items.

Julio nodded. "Whoever doesn't get a chair is out. It tests to see if you have an assertive personality."

Edgar had no problem being assertive, but he was a firm believer he could be assertive and polite. Also, he preferred to be friendly and welcoming. "But it leaves out traits like teamwork and empathy."

Julio shrugged. "You got a chair, didn't you?"

"No. I didn't. Kimbra was bidding me *adieu* when Mr. Granger stopped by and said he wanted to hire me."

The third man in the room whose desk labeled him "Armon" snorted. "Amaricio Granger has never done an impulsive thing in his life."

Though he wasn't yet an employee, Edgar felt a twinge of loyalty to the man who'd given him a job. "Most hirings are impulsive. People with identical resumes come in, and you hire them based on whether you feel like they'd fit in with the company. He just made up his mind faster."

Vander muttered something.

"I'm sorry?" Edgar hadn't been listening.

"Nothing. I'm going to go scan your ID and get you a badge. Stay here."

Julio and Armon exchanged a look.

Edgar wasn't stupid. "Okay, that's not nothing. What's going on?"

"Well, Kimbra was supposed to narrow it down to the top candidates, and then they were supposed to meet with Mr. Granger. It's strange that he came downstairs and pretty much skipped the interview process." Julio leaned forward, a conspiratorial glimmer in his eyes. "Are you connected?"

"Connected?"

"Yeah, like maybe you're *good friends* with one of the executives?" Julio winked.

Edgar didn't like the implication. "No, I'm not connected. Unless you're looking to adopt a dog. If that's the case, I can hook you up."

The spark in Julio's eyes faded. He sat up straight as Vander returned. "At any rate, congratulations and welcome to Draco International."

Vander handed him a badge. "This is your company identification. You must have it with you at all times. Once you're cleared by security, the chip in your card will be activated with your access codes. It will give you access into any area where you're allowed, which is pretty much everywhere because you have to be able to get to where Mr. Granger is."

Edgar stood. "Where is security?"

"Left out the door, down the hall to the left. Big guys, lots of tech. You can't miss it."

On his way, he sent a text to Brielle. *Got the job. Starting now. See you tonight.*

Chapter 2—Amar

"Grange, you can't hire someone without vetting them first." Ezekiel Lowry, Amaricio Granger's best friend, lounged on the black leather sofa in his office, dropping peanuts—shells and all—into his mouth.

Amaricio's friends tended to call him by his last name, or some variation thereof. His family stuck to using his first name, though they often shortened it to Amar.

"I just did." Amar flipped through a report in search of the data he needed.

"Tito is going to lose his shit."

Tito Kaysar sat at the head of the board of directors for Draco International. He was also the leader of their tribe of dragon shifters. He filled the roles of mentor and pain-in-the-ass very well. Amar ignored Zeke's prediction and his crunching.

"Grange, are you ignoring me?"

"Little bit." He found the data he needed and compared it to what was on his screen. "I'm trying to do an internal audit. The last thing we need is to fuck up our taxes and have the government getting into our business."

Draco International had been around for hundreds of years, and the company had amassed a great and diversified wealth. They used this money to maintain a relative anonymity in the world. Dragon shifters prized their privacy.

A hand came down on the glossy cover of the report, slamming it shut. Amar lifted his gaze and silently communicated displeasure. Most people would quake at the expression, but Zeke wasn't impressed.

Zeke's mouth had lines of annoyance around it, which made him look like a pouty supermodel. Thunder flashed in his blue eyes. "Tito deals with problems in ways that aren't always nice for other people."

Amar huffed. "He won't lay a hand on me. I'll rip him to shreds."

"You might, but your new little boy toy won't fare so well."

Though he understood Zeke's point, he waved away the concern. "He's not my boy toy. I don't even know if his bread is buttered on that side." Truthfully, he figured that Edgar was gay. Everything about him screamed 'twink.' However he hadn't asked, and it didn't matter anyway. That wasn't why Amar had hired him. "He's a personal assistant. Kimbra made it clear some of the things I've been asking her to do aren't under her job description. He'll be working with her to do assistant stuff that she says aren't her job."

Zeke exhaled steam. "You aren't listening. He hasn't been vetted."

Waving the steam away, Amar leaned forward. "He'll go through the vetting process, and you'll see he's clean."

"You don't know that."

To set his buddy's mind at ease, Amar told him about his encounter with Edgar in the restroom. "He had no idea who I was."

Zeke plopped into the chair opposite Amaricio's desk, and he folded his hands in his lap. "What does he look like?"

Knowing exactly where Zeke's thought were heading, Amaricio snorted. "Like a normal human. Are you actually going to work today, or have you been tasked with changing my mind? Because that's not going to happen. My assistant, my choice."

A knock at the door saved him from Zeke's attempt at a witty reply. Kimbra poked her head inside. "Mr. Granger, do you have a moment?"

He had no doubt she intended to let him know she wasn't happy about the way he'd usurped her authority. "Sure. Come on in."

She came inside, tablet in hand. "Mr. Vidal has passed his initial security check. They're asking to hold off on issuing full credentials until they can complete a deeper background check."

Amaricio threw a warning glance at Zeke. He did not need his friend adding fuel to his admin's fire. "That's fine."

"It means he won't get a phone or laptop credentials until next week at the soonest." She paused expectantly.

He hadn't expected to have an assistant quite so soon anyway. "That's inconvenient. Tell them to finish by Monday."

"Do you want Mr. Vidal to start on Monday?"

"No. He can start today. I can train him on duties that don't require a cell phone. Where is he?"

"On his way up. He got lost coming out of security. He took a wrong turn and ended up in food services." She favored him with a sour look. "Mr. Granger, far be it from me to question your choice—"

"Then don't question it." Though Amar wasn't known for being an approachable boss, Kimbra had survived with him for the past six years because she ignored his 'grumping and growling' as she called it.

"Have you looked at his resume?"

"No." He didn't need to. He knew when a person was right for a job. His instincts for finding good people were second to none.

She slipped a sheet of paper out from behind her tablet and set it on his desk. "You said I would have a say in who you hire since I'm the one who is going to have to work closely with them."

The original plan called for Kimbra to present him with four-to-six acceptable options. He'd circumvented her process, so he understood her pique. He scanned the resume, which didn't take long because there wasn't much on it. Edgar had been a dog-walker and masseur. Maybe he'd be able to take care of the tension headaches Amar tended to get when budgets were due.

Because he didn't have a good answer for Kimbra and because he disliked being questioned, he glared.

Zeke took the resume and read it over. "It looks like you're going to have to get a dog. At least your assistant will be able to give it massages."

"What?" He snatched the resume back. Either Edgar wasn't great with editing, or he had been a dog masseur. That didn't mean he couldn't also massage a neck and shoulders.

Zeke and Kimbra exchanged a look.

"Fuck off, both of you." He narrowed his eyes at Kimbra. "He's friendly. In a week, you're going to be thanking me for hiring him."

"Knock, knock—anybody here?" Edgar's voice traveled into the office.

Zeke peered through the open door into the outer office where Kimbra, and now Edgar, would be stationed. He waved. "In here."

Like a breath of fresh air, Edgar sailed into the office carrying his messenger bag and a tiny wicker basket. He crossed the room and set the basket on Amar's desk. "Mr. Granger, I'd like to thank you for this wonderful opportunity." He patted the handle of the basket. "On my way here, I stumbled into the kitchen—who knew this place had a restaurant?—and the chef was making this incredible shrimp curry. It was a new recipe, and he let me be the tester. Divine!"

His vision suddenly improved, and his hand partially morphed into a talon. In the restroom, his dragon had purred from Edgar's sweet treatment, and now it wanted more of the same. Amar covered up for the way his dragon woke up the moment Edgar entered the room by eyeing the basket doubtfully. Curry had a strong odor, and he couldn't discern anything like that coming from the basket. It smelled sugary. "Is that curry?"

"No. The curry wasn't ready, but I got you some sweet treats because I know you have a sweet tooth."

At this, Zeke perked up. As a species, dragons were drawn to sweets. He opened the basket and lifted out a crème brulee. "Oh, man. This is awesome." He headed for the door with the treat. "Good luck with avoiding Tito."

Kimbra waited, hand on hip, for instructions.

Amar cleared his throat. "Close the door and then have a seat, Kimbra. There are things for the three of us to discuss." He could have conducted the meeting without her, but he didn't trust himself to be alone with Edgar at that moment.

"Yes, Mr. Granger." She closed the door behind her a little harder than necessary. Amar chose not to react.

Edgar sat in the chair Zeke had vacated. He smoothed down a wrinkle in his khaki pants. Though he wore them well, they didn't seem like his usual attire. "Mr. Granger, can I be honest?"

"Please."

"I have no idea what this job is or why you hired me." He gestured in the direction of the outer office. "Seems like you already have an assistant, and if I'm reading her correctly, she's not sure why you hired me either."

Kimbra started. Then she set her tablet down and sat back in her chair. "I'm the office manager. Mr. Vidal, is it true your last job was as a dog masseur?"

Edgar grinned and clasped his hands together in his lap. "I volunteer at no-kill pet shelters, massaging and walking dogs. Sometimes cats—it depends on if they like me or not. It keeps their spirits up, and happy dogs are adopted faster." He reached over and touched her arm. "You can call me Edgar."

Amaricio's instincts about people were never wrong, and Kimbra was warming up to his newest acquisition. "Edgar, your job is to be my personal assistant. Kimbra will handle everything business-related, and you'll handle the rest."

He frowned. "So you hired me because I stain-sticked your tie?"

"Yes. Kimbra wouldn't have noticed the stain."

"I notice conflicts in your schedule." Spots of color flamed on her cheeks.

"Which is why you'll focus on that, and Edgar will focus on all the things you won't do."

Edgar shifted uncomfortably. "Let's be less vague about these things Kimbra won't do in case they're things I won't do either."

Amaricio hadn't expected that. Sure, he'd checked out Edgar in the restroom, but that was only because he talked about having love handles, and Amaricio couldn't find where those might have been. Edgar had a lithe body. He was small, perhaps 5'7, but he was fit.

And cute. His round face, warm brown eyes, and perpetual smile made him seem friendly and approachable. He had light brown hair with a white patch over one eye that made Amar want to run his fingers through it. Normally if someone tried to touch Amar's face, alarm bells would blare and his reflexes would kick in. When Edgar had done that, Amar's inner dragon had eagerly awaited the contact. This was a curious new development, and Amar wasn't about to let a man get away who could calm his fiery temper.

Kimbra's ire shifted to Edgar. "He's not like that." She waited three beats, and then she continued. "You're the one who has to go to his house when he somehow shows up without a sock, and get him a new pair. Or when his pant leg is torn, you'll have to run back and get another pair. I'll never understand how one man can do so much damage to his clothes on his way to work."

Though she made him sound like one, he wasn't a nitwit. Sometimes he was forced to shift unexpectedly. He tried to save his clothes as much as he could, but occasionally a wayward scale emerged early, and it ripped through his clothes. And taking off socks quickly while hopping about on the other foot—that just sucked.

"Some of the things you mentioned when we talked—occasional meal prep, picking up my dry cleaning, running errands in general—that's what I want you to do. I'll need you to be available a few evenings each week to help me get ready for dinner parties or whatever, and you'll need to be on call when I'm working through a weekend."

Edgar's brows knit together. "This seems like a lot more than an office job."

"Your hours will be irregular. Be sure to log your overtime and keep track of expenses. Next week, when you get your phone and laptop, you'll get a corporate credit card for purchases I have you make. Keep all receipts."

Kimbra's jaw fell open. "Mr. Granger, I don't think Mr. Kaysar is going to look kindly on you using a D.I. employee for personal purposes."

Amar shrugged. Tito had approved his request for a PA. "He's a personal assistant. What else is he supposed to do?"

"Help manage your schedule to minimize professional and personal conflicts, travel with you when you need to have an assistant on a business trip, run back to your house when you forget your homework, and generally help me make you look good."

He always looked good, so he resented Kimbra's implication.

"So, it's a fluid job description." Edgar chewed on his bottom lip. "What are my days off? I volunteer with the dogs, and I, you know, have a personal life."

"I don't take days off," Amaricio announced. He had a personal life? What the hell did that mean? Did Edgar have a boyfriend? Amar's dragon flamed an offer to incinerate this unknown person, and he had to look away to control it. Even if Edgar had a boyfriend, it was none of his concern.

Kimbra rolled her eyes. "Flex time. If you work on a weekend, take a day off during the week." She rose and gestured to Edgar. "Come on, Eddie. Let's get you situated."

"It's Edgar, unless you want me to call you Kimmie?"

Amaricio chuckled as he returned to the task at hand. He didn't get far when Tito Kaysar came into his office. Kimbra barely had time to warn him electronically.

He stood, greeting his mentor and boss. "Tito, it's great to see you."

"Granger, I'm not pleased with you." Tito drew his sharp brows together, making them look like an evil, gray volcano. He had sharp features, just as Amar did. Tito was his father's uncle, and so he'd been a presence in Amar's life for as long as he could remember.

While he didn't like that he'd displeased Tito, he felt the need to stand his ground. He came around his desk and gestured to the leather sofa on the opposite side of his office. "I know I broke with protocol in hiring my assistant, but I'm confident he'll pass all background checks."

Tito sank down on the comfortable leather. "I'm going to be brutally honest with you, Amaricio."

"Sure." Amar wasn't worried. Tito was often brutally honest. While most people quaked when facing this formidable man, Amar knew that behind his rough exterior, Tito had everyone's best interest at heart. It was the primary force motivating his every action.

"It was my hope you'd choose a suitable omega as your assistant."

Amar didn't need Tito to explain in order to connect the dots. "You were hoping to match me through my assistant."

"It makes sense. Omegas make for excellent assistants. They are naturally subordinate, and they want to please their alpha. If you had any chemistry whatsoever with him, then a romantic relationship would develop in due time." Tito huffed out a long breath. "It's time you were mated."

Amaricio had no interest in dating, and while he wouldn't mind having an omega around, Amar's dedication to work would leave little time for that omega. It wouldn't be fair. Of course, if this omega was also his assistant, then it made sense that he'd get to spend more time with him.

All-in-all, Tito had a solid plan.

And yet, Amar couldn't seem to muster enthusiasm for it. "If Edgar doesn't work out, we'll try your plan."

With an aggravated sigh, Tito got to his feet. "I need not remind you a human is not a suitable choice for a mate."

Frankly, Amar didn't care. He wasn't looking for a mate in the first place, and in the second place, he hadn't hired Edgar to keep a piece of ass nearby.

An hour later, he called Kimbra into his office. "The bids from Brazil, Mexico, Germany, and Canada should be in by now."

She took notes as she listened. "Do you want the bids from Colorado and Kentucky as well?"

Draco International liked to keep their supply chain separated so nobody quite knew all the components of the final product. Their latest project had defense applications and could net them a huge government contract. "Sure."

A noise, blissful and slightly sexual in nature, came through the open door. Amar frowned, mostly because it made his dragon stir. "What's going on out there?"

"Edgar found the supply cupboard. He has a thing for sticky notes."

"Sticky notes?"

"Yes, Mr. Granger. Sticky notes. He's appropriated all sorts of colors and sizes, and he has lined them up on his desk."

It wasn't as if Amar had given Edgar a specific task yet. "Give him something to do. Have him help you out."

Kimbra pressed her lips together and inhaled. "Mr. Granger, you got an assistant for you, not for me. You give him something to do."

He thought through his mental list for things he'd like for Kimbra to do that she would balk at. "Send him in."

Seconds later, Edgar bounded in. "What can I do for you, Mr. Granger?"

"Make dinner reservations for me and Mr. Lowry at Benevolence."

"For tonight?"

"Yes." That would keep him busy for a while. Benevolence almost never had an opening on short notice.

Edgar rubbed his hands together. "Anything else?"

He handed over a ticket. "Get my dry cleaning."

"I'm on it, Mr. Granger." With a grin, he snatched up the ticket and left the room.

Did Amar imagine everything seemed dimmer after he'd gone?

Chapter 3—Edgar

Working for Amaricio Granger wasn't like any job Edgar had held before—and he'd held a lot of them. Most didn't make it to his resume because Brielle said too much made him seem flaky, like he couldn't hold down a job.

The truth of the matter was Edgar didn't keep a job for very long. He inevitably got wrapped up in minutiae and forgot about the task at hand. That led employers to show him the door—always regretfully because people genuinely seemed to like him.

He decided to put extra effort into completing tasks for Mr. Granger. This job paid well. Maybe he'd be able to help Brielle out with her fostering costs.

First he looked up Benevolence on his phone. He'd never heard of it before. When he called, they said they had no open reservations, so he went for the dry cleaning.

Since it was a nice day and Edgar didn't have a car, he walked to the cleaners. On the way, a large dog whipped past him, leash streaming behind like a banner of freedom. Down the street, a woman screeched for the dog to stop. Without another thought, Edgar ran after the dog.

The dog was starting to tire, so Edgar got into a loping jog and came up alongside the canine.

"Hey," he said. "Nice day for a run."

The dog, a brindle-coated mutt, made sounds, some whines and growls Edgar interpreted as playful.

"I'm Edgar. What's your name?"

Glancing over, the dog seemed to communicate his name was Herbie.

"Herbie, do you think it's nice to run away when she's wearing high heels? She could hurt herself."

At that, the dog stopped. He faced Edgar with his head bowed.

"Good boy." Edgar stroked the dog's head and took the leash. "Remember—no more running away when she's wearing heels. If she has tennis shoes on, then go for it. You have to pay attention to these things."

He returned the dog to the woman. "Here you go. I've had a chat with him. He's going to be good while you're wearing heels."

She took the leash, and then she crouched down and scratched behind Herbie's ears. "That's my good little boy. Oh, you scare me when you do that. I'm afraid you're going to get hit by a car—or worse."

"He needs to run. There's a dog park a few streets over, on Ninth, that he'd like."

The woman stood up. In those heels, she towered over Edgar by a few inches, and her smile was friendly. "Are you a doggie daddy?"

"Not right now. My sister fosters dogs, and I do dog walking. I take them to the park quite often. It's fun."

She lowered her sunglasses and appraised him with new eyes. He noticed they were gold in the sunlight, and they matched her hair. "You're a dog walker? Are you for hire?"

This is the part where Edgar usually got in trouble. If he accepted a job from this lady, then it would somehow interfere with his job for Mr. Granger, and he'd end up disappointing both of them. He smiled regretfully, a look Brielle claimed won hearts. "Sorry. I'm not. Right now, I'm picking up dry cleaning for my boss, and then I'm going to try to get reservations at an exclusive restaurant for tonight."

The woman frowned. "Sounds like your boss is expecting the impossible."

Edgar lifted a shoulder. "Maybe I'll be back to walking dogs next week. I like dogs, so that's not a hardship."

She dug in her purse and handed over her card. "If you find yourself out of work, call me."

He glanced at it before tucking it into his trusty messenger bag. It identified Brenna Goodrich, attorney. "Thanks, Ms. Goodrich. I hope you and Herbie have a great day."

"Herbie?" She glanced around.

"Your dog?"

"His name is Jefferson."

The dog coughed his disapproval.

"Sorry. I thought I heard you call him Herbie." Edgar lifted a hand to wave as he took his leave. "It was nice to meet you both."

He collected the dry cleaning. On the way back, he ducked into Benevolence to try again for a reservation. The front door was locked, so he went around back to the service entrance. Staff bustled around, prepping food and such.

Edgar jumped out of the way twice before the chef noticed he was there.

The large man with no hair glared. "You—what are you doing here? Get out of my kitchen."

"Me?" Edgar pointed to himself.

"Edgar? Is that you?" An assistant cook wiped his hands on a towel and scurried over. "Holy cow—it is you. What are you doing here? How have you been?"

It took Edgar a moment, but he recognized Hector, a man with whom he'd enjoyed a brief fling. With his free arm, he hugged the man. "Hector, it's been a while. I'm fabulous, and you're finally a chef. How exciting for you."

"Yes, it is." His eyes twinkled.

"Hector, get that guy out of here—pronto." The chef shot a nasty look through narrowed eyes.

"Don't mind him. He's all bark and no bite." Hector giggled. "Seriously, though, what are you doing here?"

"I need to make a reservation for my boss and his associate tonight. I was in the neighborhood, so I thought I'd stop by instead of calling."

Hector's eyes widened. "Edgar, this is the sort of place where you get reservations months in advance."

With a laugh, Edgar touched Hector's shoulder. "I just got the job today. I'd hate to lose it. Plus now I want to taste your cooking."

"Yeah?" Hector perked up. "Will you be there too?"

"If you can hook me up with a table for three?"

Hector pushed him into a hallway near the back entrance. "Wait here. I'll see what I can do."

Edgar slung the dry cleaning over his shoulder and waited. It didn't take long for Hector to return.

His bottom lip was pouty. "I could only get a table for two. I put the reservation under your name." He leaned closer. "I'll send something special home for you. I remember how much you love a doggy bag."

He returned to the office victorious. Kimbra sighed when he came in. One day he'd win her over. It would happen one smile at a time. "Hi, Kimbra. Where should I put Mr. Granger's dry cleaning?"

She motioned to his office. "I'm not getting involved with his clothes."

Edgar knocked on the door and was met with a gruff order to enter. He found Mr. Granger standing in front of the window reading a sheaf of papers. Energy poured from the man, and Edgar was reminded of his initial impression—this was a man who got things done. And who had a very fine ass. Without his jacket on, Edgar had an unobstructed view of those rounded, muscular cheeks and the thickness of Mr. Granger's thighs. His boss was handsome and built.

Edgar ripped his appreciative gaze away before Mr. Granger caught him gawking. Figuring the boss man was busy with something important, he set the suits he'd picked up over the back of a chair. Then he got a sticky note from his messenger bag and wrote down the details for Mr. Granger's dinner at Benevolence.

When he would have crept out, Mr. Granger's voice stopped him. "In the future, unless I say otherwise, I want you to take my clothes home and hang them up."

"Home? To my place?"

Mr. Granger's gaze lifted slowly so Edgar had time to contemplate the stupidity of his question.

"Sorry. I don't know where you live. Also, I'm going to need a key."

"Clearance." His lips thinned. "Once security is finished with your background check, they'll activate your badge, which will let you into my apartment."

"Oh. That's handy. And also strange."

"Strange?"

"I mean, that your workplace would provide the security for your house. You know what? Not my business. Shutting up now."

If he wasn't mistaken, Mr. Granger almost smiled. "Were you able to get a table at Benevolence?"

"Yes. I had to sleep with the chef's assistant, but I got you a reservation for two at eight-thirty. It's under my name."

Boss man's body became eerily still, which set off warning bells in Edgar. He straightened his spine and attuned his senses to find any threat. He heard nothing, but the hypervigilant state made him very aware of just how good Mr. Granger smelled. Edgar wouldn't mind burying his nose in that man's body.

Finally, Mr. Granger moved. He set the paper he'd been reading on his desk and stopped less than a foot away from Edgar. His nostrils flared, matching the fire in his eyes. "You had sex with the chef's assistant to get a reservation for me?" He spoke softly, but there was no mistaking his fury.

"I was kidding." Sort of. He had slept with the chef's assistant, only that had happened at least a year ago. For some reason, he didn't want to disclose that he'd been intimate with Hector. He sensed Mr. Granger wasn't the kind of person who wanted to know his sexual history. "He's an old friend."

Again, Mr. Granger looked like he was sniffing Edgar. He didn't move or anything, and it was mostly Edgar's sixth sense picking up the action. Caught in some kind of spell, Edgar swayed toward the powerful, attractive man. He stopped before he embarrassed himself. *Do not fall into the arms of a man who is frowning at you, Edgar. It's not going to bring a smile to his face.*

Abruptly Mr. Granger moved away. "In the future, refrain from that sort of humor."

"Sure thing."

"Close the door on your way out."

Edgar did that, and he sagged against it in the safety of Kimbra's office.

She glanced up. "He has a reputation for being a dragon, but I've found if he knows you're on his side, he's mostly a pussy cat."

"Good to know he's not going to roast me and have me for dinner. He'll just flay me with his claws." He sank down behind the empty desk that was now his and pulled out a stack of sticky notes stuck end-to-end so they lifted up in a pretty pattern. "Please tell me he has a sense of humor."

"Not that I've seen."

"Does he smile?"

"Mostly when the numbers work out like he wants." Kimbra favored him with a sympathetic click of her tongue. "What happened?"

"He didn't like my joke about sleeping with the chef's assistant to get him a reservation at Benevolence."

Her typing fingers paused. "You got a reservation there on short notice?"

"I did."

"And you didn't sleep with the chef's assistant?"

He shrugged. "Not recently."

She opened and closed her mouth. "Last week the company made us all go to a sexual harassment seminar. They have a hardline policy about that kind of thing. Mr. Granger was probably concerned he was responsible for a violation."

"Oh. Well, Hector and I went out a few times a long time ago. We're still on friendly terms. He got Mr. Granger in as a favor to me."

Kimbra sighed again. "Edgar, when you call to make reservations, be sure to give Mr. Granger's full name and title. You'll find there is suddenly a table available at most establishments, though Benevolence still takes some bartering to convince."

"Thanks for the tip." He winked, certain he and Kimbra were on their way to becoming friends. "Hey, Kimbra," he whispered. "On a scale of one to ten, what do you rate Mr. Granger's ass?"

Her eyes widened in alarm, and her gaze went to the door between them that led to their boss's office. "Remember the sexual harassment seminar I told you about?"

It hadn't been that long ago. "Yes."

"I think maybe you need to go to it."

He rolled his eyes. "If you don't swing that way, just tell me. Sheesh. I give it a nine."

"Nine?" Despite her disapproval, she appeared to have an opinion on the matter. "Why not a ten?"

"Nobody's perfect."

Chapter 4—Amar

Being a dragon shifter meant he had excellent hearing. Before Edgar had arrived in the outer office, he'd never paid much attention to the murmurings coming from that direction. Now he heard with crystal clarity Edgar's opinion of his ass.

"Perfect," he muttered. "I'll show you perfect."

Edgar's comment about sleeping with the chef's assistant rankled, and listening in on the conversation between his assistants helped him to understand why. It hadn't really been uttered in jest. Edgar had a past relationship with the man who would be cooking for Amar. Jealousy surged through him, and he struggled to tamp it down. He had no reason for the emotion. Edgar was his employee, not his lover. As Tito had said, a human was not a suitable mate for a shifter.

Still he considered canceling the reservation.

That night, he met Zeke in the lobby of the restaurant. His buddy waited, drink in hand, and listened to a woman who was openly flirting. She leaned closer, not noticing how Zeke leaned away. She had no idea she was barking up the wrong tree.

He lifted his hand, signaling to Zeke and asking if his fellow sharp-winged dragon needed help disengaging from the unwanted attention.

Zeke got free all by himself. He approached with a regretful air. "They're saying they don't have a reservation under your name. We can go to my club."

"It's under Edgar's name." As Amar steered Zeke toward the maître d', he wondered if perhaps Edgar had been mistaken about the details. "Two for eight-thirty. Vidal."

The man in a suit jacket beamed. "You're Mr. Vidal?"

"No. I'm Amaricio Granger, CFO of Draco International. Mr. Vidal is my assistant. He made the reservation."

"My apologies for the mix-up. Let me show you to your table."

Despite his earlier inclination, he enjoyed his meal with Zeke. As they finished off the last of the bottle of wine, the server brought out a white paper bag. On the side, someone had drawn a cartoon dog with a slobbery smile and a wagging tail.

Amar eyed it curiously. "What's this?"

"I'm not sure, Mr. Granger. The pastry chef told me to bring it to your table. He said you'd know what to do with it."

He realized the pastry chef was probably the one Edgar had relied upon for this reservation. Amar's expression turned to stone as he thought about the decadent cheesecake he'd just eaten and the fact it had been prepared by Edgar's former lover. He wanted to get a look at the guy, see what kind of man revved his attractive assistant's engine.

Zeke had always been great at realizing the drift of Amar's thoughts. "Thank you." He closed his hand over the folded top. "I ordered extra dessert."

Amar threw cash on the table. "Let's go."

He tried to snatch the bag from Zeke, but his buddy held it out of reach, and going for it would create a disturbance in this upscale setting.

Once they were on the sidewalk, all bets were off. Zeke backed up, holding the bag behind his back.

"Give it to me." Amar held out a hand.

"Not until you tell me why it's pissing you off."

He didn't want to tell Zeke about the inexplicable emotions rioting inside him for no apparent reason. "Give me the fucking bag."

Zeke handed it over. "It smells like cheesecake. Maybe Edgar ordered you one for the road? He did bring you crème brulee today."

"That you ate." Amar tore open the bag. Inside was a white container with a note scribbled on it in black ink. *E—It was great seeing you today. Here's a doggie bag for a sexy animal. Call me sometime. I miss you. xoxo—H.*

Then there was a phone number.

"I need a fucking drink." He shoved the container inside the bag.

Zeke took it before he could crumple it up and toss it into a city receptacle. "Luckily there's a pub next door."

Two hours later, he found himself seated in a booth across from Zeke. The world wobbled blearily in front of him.

"My dragon likes him," he said to Zeke. "It purrs. It fucking purrs."

"I'm sure you don't find him at all attractive."

"He's a twink."

"Delicate. Sensitive. Human."

"Full of delicious cream."

"Not a shifter." Zeke threw some cold water on the fire. "Good for a fling, though."

They knew all the dragon shifters in the area, and Edgar wasn't one of them. Plus, as a rule, fully grown dragon shifters were larger, well over six feet tall. Amar and Zeke were both 6'6, which was average height among their kind. How could his dragon lust after a non-shifter so relentlessly? Perhaps it would simmer down if he threw a quick one-night stand at it?

"Mr. Granger?"

He looked up to see Edgar in the server's place. He wore a dark blue shirt with a dog on it, and on the bottom half, he wore sweatpants. They rode low on his hips. That leather messenger bag was slung across his chest.

Zeke got up. "I'm going home. See you tomorrow." He clapped a hand on Edgar's shoulder. "Take him home."

"I will, Mr. Lowry. How are you getting home?"

"I called for a ride. Don't worry about me." Zeke threw money on the table and disappeared.

Amar scooted to the edge of the booth seat. The world tilted as he got to his feet, and when things made sense again, Edgar's arm was around his waist and they were outside the restaurant.

"I've got you, Mr. Granger. Let's get you home." He grinned up at Amar. "I guess this is one of the things Kimbra doesn't want to do for you."

He'd never considered calling Kimbra when he wasn't at work. For that matter, he hadn't considered calling Edgar; he'd considered finding out where he lived so he could show him what it was like to be kissed by a real man.

"I didn't call you." He heard the slur in his words. "Zeke did."

"Well, in that case, let me sit you on a park bench and leave you here." Edgar slung him onto a bench at the bus stop they were passing.

Amar grabbed for Edgar, throwing his arms around the twink's waist. He buried his face in the smaller man's stomach and inhaled. His dragon purred.

"I was kidding." Edgar stroked his fingers through Amar's hair. "You're heavy. I need a break. Note to self: Drunk or sober, Mr. Granger does not appreciate my sense of humor."

Jealousy streaked through Amar's veins, negating some of the alcohol. Rising to his feet, he withdrew the crushed dessert container from his pocket and shoved it at Edgar. "It's not humor when you fuck a pastry chef to get me a reservation."

The twinkle extinguished from Edgar's eye, replaced by wariness. He looked at the object Amar had put in his hands. The inscription on the package was still readable. He tossed the ruined dessert into a nearby trash can. Dusting off his hands, he returned to where Amar waited.

"Come on, Mr. Granger. Let's get you home. Do you have any cash? I could call for a ride."

He blinked at Edgar, wondering at the change in tone.

Then Edgar's hands were on him, his palm sliding along Amar's chest. His heart stuttered before beating harder. Acting on instinct alone, he pulled the smaller man to him and mashed his lips against Edgar's.

Edgar's body stiffened, but he didn't otherwise resist. His hands even stopped roaming.

Amar's instincts abandoned him as his better sense took over. Slowly he put Edgar down. "Sorry. That was wrong of me."

"Yeah." Edgar moved back a step. He opened Amar's wallet. "I was just going for your wallet to see if you had cash. You do. I'll call for a ride."

Fifteen minutes later, Amar found himself in the backseat of a car with Edgar next to him. Edgar read the address from Amar's identification, and the two sat in silence.

They arrived at their destination, and Edgar helped Amar out of the car. He paid the driver. Amar watched the tail lights of the car fade into the distance. "You could have had him drive you home."

"What kind of assistant would I be if I didn't make sure you got to your apartment safely?" Edgar slung an arm around Amar's waist. "Come on, Mr. Granger. We're almost there."

The night doorman opened the door to admit them. "Good evening, Mr. Granger."

"Hi, Nate. This is Edgar Vidal, my assistant. Put him on the list, and get him a key." A key would work without the security badge.

"Very good, Mr. Granger."

In the elevator, he leaned against the wall and willed himself to get his shit together. He was an alpha dragon. Edgar was supposed to be his assistant. Maybe he wasn't an omega, but he definitely had submissive tendencies, which was one of the things Amar liked about him.

When the elevator doors slid open, Edgar reached for Amar again, but Amar jerked from his grasp. There was only so much handling he could stand from the not-omega before his alpha side took over. "I'm fine. I can do it."

Edgar trailed after him, not commenting when Amar stumbled or when he knocked over a potted plant in front of a window at the end of the hall.

Amar scanned his fingerprint to unlock the door to his place. Inside the foyer, he searched his jacket for his wallet.

"What do you need, Mr. Granger?"

"My wallet. I was going to give you some cash so you could get a ride home."

Edgar held it up. "I have your wallet." He closed the door behind him. "Why did you smash up the dessert Hector gave to you for me?"

At the mention of the pastry chef, Amar grasped Edgar by his shirt and hauled him closer. He was warm and his unique aroma invaded Amar's senses. "You said my ass was a nine."

Edgar exhaled and pressed his lips together. "If it helps, Hector's ass is only a four."

It shouldn't help, but it did. Some of the jealousy eased. He released his hold on Edgar's shirt.

"That doesn't explain why you would ruin a perfectly good slice of cheesecake. I love cheesecake."

It occurred to Amar that Edgar might be kidding. After all, he'd misconstrued both jokes Edgar had attempted today. Rather than respond, he stumbled to the bedroom, shedding his clothes along the way.

He went into the bathroom in the master suite and came out wearing only his boxers. Edgar stood in the center of the room, looking around.

"What are you doing?"

"Looking for your laundry hamper. I didn't think you wanted your clothes left on the floor."

The room was large, but Amar's legs were long. He ate up the distance between them and snatched the bundle from Edgar. "You can go. I told you to take money from my wallet to pay your fare." The laundry basket was in the closet, so he went in that direction.

"Mr. Granger, I'm still waiting for an answer. The cheesecake didn't do anything to you."

"You're serious?" He stopped, and he turned the fire of his most menacing glare on Edgar. "You want cheesecake? I'll buy you a fucking cheesecake." He flung the ball of his clothes away and looked toward the dresser where he normally kept his billfold. "Where did you put my wallet?"

"On the table in the hall." Edgar set his hands on his hips, bringing Amar's attention to those delightfully narrow hips. "Mr. Granger, I'm not leaving until you tell me why you're behaving so badly. You're like a jealous boyfriend."

Amar agreed with Edgar's assessment, but he didn't have an explanation. Backing an apex predator into a corner was never a good idea. On stealthy feet, he approached Edgar. The handsome man gazed up at him with limpid pools of melted chocolate. He badly wanted a taste.

"If you don't leave right now, I'm not going to be responsible for my actions."

Edgar's gaze traveled down Amar's body, openly appreciating the view. "Mr. Granger, you're so drunk I could light your breath on fire with a match. You might be bigger than me, but I'm sober, and you can barely stand up. Go brush your teeth so I can put you to bed."

A match wasn't necessary to light Amar's breath on fire, since he was a fire-breathing dragon and all. He gripped Edgar's head in his hand, tilting the smaller man's face to the perfect angle, and then his lips captured Edgar's. A shock of recognition shot straight to his dragon. It whined and purred, bubbling to the surface.

Edgar's lips parted, and Amar took full advantage of the invitation. He tasted sweet and hot. Amar's arms snaked around Edgar as he lifted him to alleviate the height difference. His tongue morphed because he couldn't suppress the primal part of him that lusted for a taste. Edgar kissed him back enthusiastically, not noticing the small differences.

Amar's claws came next, and he shredded Edgar's shirt in his effort to pull it off of him. The pair tumbled to the bed. Edgar's palms skated over Amar's flesh, leaving streaks of quaking pleasure in their wake. He needed to taste every inch of this man, so he broke away from kissing Edgar's mouth to trail kisses and licks down his body.

"You are one fucking hot twink."

"Not a twink." Edgar writhed as Amar's tongue circled his nipple. "I work out and have muscle definition. I like to run or walk, and I'm great at catch or Frisbee. Cub, maybe."

"Sexy as fuck," Amar amended. He slid Edgar's sweatpants down, and his cock popped out. The cub wasn't wearing underwear. Amar groaned as he licked the length of Edgar's erection.

Edgar hissed. "Mr. Granger, that feels so good."

Amar growled. "Use my first name."

"Amaricio, that feels so good." The name rolled from Edgar's lips and stoked Amar's desire.

"Again, Edgar. I want to hear you cry out my name when you come." With that, he took Edgar's cock fully in his mouth. He tasted like sunshine and sweetness with a musky hint of passion. Amar had never sampled anything quite so wonderful before.

He sucked harder, setting a furious rhythm. Sounds of pleasure mingled with moans of his name made Amar's dick pulse. As he increased the pace of the blowjob, he took his own cock in hand.

"Amaricio, oh, Amaricio." Edgar's hips moved, and he clutched the plush bedspread beneath him. "I'm close. I'm so close."

Amar wrapped his long, forked tongue around Edgar's dick. As he sucked, he flicked the end against the sensitive spot under the crown. With a guttural cry, Edgar climaxed. His semen spurted into Amar's mouth, and he eagerly sucked it down. The unique flavor triggered his own orgasm.

He flopped onto the bed next to Edgar, utterly spent. His body felt boneless and oddly sated. He smiled. "Creamy filling."

Chapter 5

Edgar

He entered the small, rented house as quietly as he could, but it turned out not to matter. Two dogs barked, and a third whimpered from behind the TV stand. Brielle sat up on the sofa. Her eyes were closed, and soft music tinkled from the television. He shut it off while petting all three dogs, and she struggled to open her eyes.

"Hey. You're back." She smiled sleepily and got to her feet.

"You didn't have to wait up." He felt bad because he knew she had to work in the morning. He opened his arms, and she fell into them. She was everything that defined the idea of home, and he hugged her tightly.

"I worry about you." Her words were sleep-slurred.

"Back at you."

She righted herself and yawned. "So what happened?"

"My boss got drunk, so I had to get him home and in bed."

"Oh." Brielle scrunched up her face. Growing up in foster care the way they had, they both distrusted drunks. "Was he an asshole?"

"Not any more than usual. It turned out that Hector sent home a slice of cheesecake for me, but Mr. Granger didn't want to give it to me." Edgar was still a little miffed about the cheesecake. He loved food, especially the kind prepared by an exclusive chef at a five-star restaurant. "So he mashed it up in his pocket and went out for drinks with his friend."

"Why would he do that?"

"I joked today that I slept with Hector to get him a reservation at Benevolence. Mr. Granger got jealous or something." He toyed with the idea of not telling Brielle the rest, but then he rejected it. He told her everything. "He gave me a blowjob."

"Hector?" Brielle frowned. "I don't remember him."

"He was like two dates last summer. We fooled around, but nothing came of it. I met James soon after."

"Bastard who broke your heart."

"That's the one." He chuckled. "I'm over him."

"Are you and Hector back together?"

"No, not Hector—Mr. Granger. I took him home, and he kissed me. One thing led to another, and the next thing I know, he's sucking me off. Then he fell asleep. I covered him up, turned off the lights, and came home." He'd left a sticky note telling Mr. Granger exactly how much money he'd taken to pay for the ride home. It was a receipt of sorts. "I think I like this job."

Brielle rolled her eyes. "You be careful. This guy sounds like he's a little off his rocker. Also, he might expect you to have sex with him as part of the job. That's wrong, Edgar. You don't have to do that. If you lose this job, we'll make it work. When we're together, we always land on our feet."

"Noted." He wasn't sure he agreed with Brielle, but he knew better than to argue with her until he understood his own thoughts on the issue of Mr. Granger. Then there was the fact Edgar tended to lose his jobs rather easily while Brielle had been a home health care provider for the past seven years. She dreamed of becoming a geriatric nurse, but classes were too expensive right now. She was the rock in their relationship. Though he was a butterfly by nature, he was often the leech when it came to his generous sister. He wanted to change their dynamic. Brielle deserved to not have to work so hard all the time.

The next morning, he slept in. While it was officially his first full day on the job, he'd put in late hours, and he was tired. He rolled in at eleven, an hour before lunch.

Kimbra was on the phone, but she glared loud enough to hear the growl.

He set his messenger bag on his desk and smiled at the tiny spitfire who reminded him a lot of Brielle. Both women were petite. They both had dark hair and fiery eyes, though Kimbra had blue eyes and Brielle's were brown. They both had great skin. Kimbra's looked as smooth and soft as Brielle's, but there was no way in hell he was going to test out that theory. She'd eat him for breakfast.

She hung up the phone. "You're late. Mr. Granger asked where you were twice already."

"I had to work last night for three hours, so I came in later this morning. Flex time, just like you said."

With a huff, she pointed at the closed door separating the offices. "You need to notify him and me when you're going to take your time off. He's in a horrible mood. Good luck not getting your head bit off."

Edgar took a pad of sticky notes and a pen with him. He also grabbed his thermos. He knocked, and Mr. Granger's curt, "Enter," crashed into the heavy wood.

Kimbra shook her head. "Apologize. Don't say anything to set him off. I've seen him fire people for less."

With that dire warning echoing in his ears, Edgar went inside. He faced Mr. Granger with a bright smile. "How's the hangover?"

"I'm not hung over." Mr. Granger scowled, which made his rugged face look downright menacing.

Except Edgar kept seeing that handsome visage flushed with passion. He vividly remembered the feel of Amaricio's lips moving against his. Someone with that fiery nature would be driven to extremes, but Edgar didn't have to react to the mercurial parts of Mr. Granger's personality. He could be a moderating influence.

Still smiling, he set the thermos on Mr. Granger's desk. Then he opened the lid and poured the contents inside. "Drink this. You'll feel better."

"I feel fine." Mr. Granger—Amaricio—insisted with words, but his attitude told a different story.

Edgar waited.

The silence wore on Mr. Granger's nerves first. He peered into the lid. "What is that?"

"Brielle's chicken soup. It's good for what ails you."

"Who the fuck is Brielle?"

"My sister, and I'll thank you not to use the F-word in the same sentence as her name. She's sweet and gentle and good-hearted." Edgar had patience for almost anything, just not where his sister was concerned.

Mr. Granger sniffed the soup. Then he drank it down. "It's good."

"I know. She's amazing."

"Why were you late today?" He poured another lid full of soup and sipped it.

"Comp time. I worked for three hours last night." He didn't count that last half hour. "Don't you remember?"

"I remember." Mr. Granger handed a card across the table. "Complaints should be registered here, with the legal department."

Edgar peered at the card. "Complaints?"

"Yes. You're well within your rights to sue the company. I will corroborate any accusations you make." His gaze landed everywhere but on Edgar.

Edgar set the card back on Mr. Granger's desk. "No, thank you. I'd prefer to keep my job the way it is."

Mr. Granger frowned. "I was out of line. You could get a huge settlement for this."

"I'd rather not." Edgar folded his arms. "You owe me a slice of cheesecake. That's all I want."

"It can't happen again."

While Edgar found the powerful man very attractive, and he wouldn't mind exploring the chemistry between them, he needed the job more than he needed a lover. "Agreed. Also, you can't treat cheesecake like that. It's a travesty, what you did to it."

He kept his shredded Dog Rescue shirt in a plastic bag in his messenger bag as a reminder he didn't know what he was dealing with where Mr. Granger was concerned. And Brielle's chicken soup was there to keep him focused on the important things—saving enough money so she could realize her dream of becoming a geriatric nurse.

"You're really upset about the cheesecake?" A crease appeared between Mr. Granger's brows, which was not a new look for him.

"Yes," Edgar said. "I love cheesecake."

A week later, Edgar had a magnetic ID card that would let him into most areas at Draco International so he could run errands for Mr. Granger. He also had a company credit card, and he had to track his purchases for his boss, labeling them personal or professional so the company could bill correctly.

After that first night, Mr. Granger kept a stoic presence around him. Kimbra said his behavior wasn't out of the ordinary, but she did admit it was a little impersonal even for him.

Edgar knew the cause, but he kept his mouth shut. The world didn't need to know his boss had given him a blowjob he mentally replayed in the shower nearly every day.

"Edgar, get in here." Mr. Granger's voice came through the speaker on the phone the tech department had installed on his desk. It had a lot of buttons and no manual to show how to work it. When

Edgar was bored, he looked online for how to work the features and what the flashing buttons meant, but so far he hadn't found anything.

A sleek computer had also appeared on his desk, and a woman from IT had helped him create a username and password to access files any employees from Draco International shared with him. This was a Job, not just a job.

Jumping to his feet, Edgar went into the large inner office. For a change, Mr. Granger sat on the leather sofa in the opposite corner from his desk. He looked up from the papers spread in front of him.

"I want to have a dinner party next Friday." He rattled off a list of people to invite.

Edgar scrambled to get all the names written on the tablet-sized sticky note he'd brought with him. "What theme were you thinking?"

Mr. Granger looked up for the first time since Edgar had entered his office. Confusion furrowed his brow. "Theme? Oh—you mean the menu. Meat is good. You can go with steak. We're not a fancy group."

Rich people prided themselves on their rich palates, or so Edgar had concluded from watching them on television. Even the restaurant in the building served fancy stuff like duck and lots of things with non-English names. He couldn't understand why they said *haricot vert* when they meant green beans.

Whatever.

"No, Mr. Granger, I meant the theme. Is this a celebration of some sort, or is it a business meeting? What's the topic of your get-together?"

Mr. Granger frowned, an expression that looked remarkably similar to his scowl. "No theme. It's just dinner."

Edgar rolled his eyes. "A dinner party is your chance to show your guests how much better you are at entertaining than they are." He heaved a heavy sigh. "I guess this is why you have me. I'll take care of the theme. What's my budget?"

"Keep it reasonable."

Reasonable was a subjective word. Edgar took that to mean he shouldn't go too far over the top. However, when he found out he could rent a round table painted to look like stone, he went with a King Arthur theme. After all, Mr. Granger planned on having twelve guests.

He printed invitations, sealed them in wax, and imprinted the Draco International insignia—a dragon—onto the warm wax. Then he hand-delivered them to each recipient.

Most of the attendees were people in the building, but a few were people Edgar hadn't yet met. When he delivered one across town at a business that supplied Draco International with parts, or maybe they built something—Edgar wasn't sure—a well-dressed woman in high heels stopped him in the lobby.

"If it isn't the man who has an extraordinary way with dogs!" She held out her hands.

Though he didn't recognize the woman, he took her hands because it seemed like the thing to do.

She kissed his cheeks, tickling his nose with the scent of expensive perfume. "Jefferson has been wonderful ever since you had a talk with him."

Edgar was still on the scent she wore. It was different from anything he'd smelled before, and often he remembered people by how they smelled. He caught no trace of dog scent on her, which was a shame. Every morning, Edgar spent time with the dogs Brielle fostered. Though he showered, he always retained the faint aroma of puppy. It calmed him and made him feel relaxed.

Then he remembered Jefferson. That was the dog he'd stopped from leading his owner on a casual jog. He preferred to be called Herbie, but people often didn't know how to listen to dogs. "I'm glad that he's stopped running away from you."

"So am I. I take him to the dog park every other day, and he seems happier. Thank you so much, and if you ever want a job, it's open."

He had a job he liked despite the fact his boss had a gruff exterior. "Your perfume smells really pretty." He didn't lie. It had undertones of flowers, but it didn't overpower his senses—which was saying something because he had a great sense of smell.

"Oh, you." She squeezed his hands and let them drop. "Come with me."

He held up an envelope. "I have to deliver this."

She read the name on it. "Jeanne Goodrich. That's my wife. It looks like an invitation."

"My employer, Amaricio Granger, is having a dinner party. He's invited Ms. Goodrich and spouse over for dinner next Friday evening." He kept the invitation because his job was to deliver it to the person bearing the name on the envelope. Mr. Granger couldn't remember Ms. Goodrich's spouse's name, so it wasn't there. Edgar figured it was a business dinner because if someone invited over a friend, they generally knew their spouse's name.

"Granger?" Brenna Goodrich—Edgar finally recalled her name— tapped her lower lip. "That name doesn't ring a bell."

"He's the CFO of Draco International."

She laughed, a musical sound, and she slid her arm through Edgar's. "That rings a bell. Goodrich Scents is developing a unique scent that will be used in their new line of diffusers. I have not met Mr. Granger. Mostly we've dealt with Koren Tafari."

"He's invited as well." Edgar allowed her to lead him into an elevator.

"Jeanne is going to love meeting you. We're both amazed at how much better behaved Jefferson has been." Her smile widened. "He's our fur baby, you know—the center of our world. He's upstairs right now."

As soon as the elevator opened, the dog in question bounded over to them. He nuzzled Brenna, his tail wagging at a million miles an hour, and then he greeted Edgar. Edgar bent down to greet the dog he still thought of as Herbie. "Hey, boy. I hear you've been behaving."

Herbie licked his chin.

A woman came next. She seemed tall, but that could have been because Edgar was crouched down or because she wore one of those dresses with a really long skirt that seemed to add height to some women and make others look even shorter. She had a friendly face with lines that showed she smiled a lot, and her eyes sparkled with happiness.

She greeted Brenna with a kiss. "I didn't expect you back so soon."

"I was on my way out when I ran into this darling young man, and I had to bring him up here to meet you. Jeanne, this is Edgar, the person who caught Jefferson and gave him a stern talking-to."

Edgar got to his feet, and he decided Jeanne was tall. She towered over Edgar by at least six inches, which was not all due to her high heels. "Hi, Ms. Goodrich. It's nice to meet you." He didn't add that if either of them ever put on tennis shoes, all bets were off.

"Edgar, I don't know how you did it, but Jefferson has been much happier since his run-in with you." She clasped his hand between hers in a warm handshake. "Call me Jeanne."

Heat crept up Edgar's neck. He'd only told Herbie not to run when his humans were in heels. "I didn't do anything much, but I'm glad you guys are getting along so well."

"You must come to dinner," Jeanne said. "I won't take no for an answer."

For some reason, dog people always took to Edgar. He wasn't sure why, but since he tended to like them back, he didn't mind. "Um, sure. I really came by to invite you to dinner, though. My employer, Amaricio Granger, CFO of Draco International, would like you to come to his place next Friday for an amazing dinner."

Jeanne took the invitation. She smiled at the wax seal. "It's the little things that mean so much."

Edgar beamed under the praise even though she hadn't necessarily aimed it in his direction. He waited as she read the details.

"Modern Knights? That's an interesting theme." She glanced up. "This sounds like fun. Will you be there?"

Assistants didn't merit a seat at the table. "Yes, but not as a guest. My job is to make sure everything goes smoothly."

"You're Mr. Granger's personal assistant?" Brenna appraised him while she asked the question.

"Yes."

"I see. Listen, Edgar, if you ever get tired of working there, my door is always open. I'm serious—we can use someone with your people skills." Brenna followed with a smile. "No pressure. In the meantime, let me get your number, and I'll be in touch to set up dinner plans."

In the elevator, when they were alone, Brenna giggled.

"What's funny?"

"I started out as Jeanne's assistant. She stole me from Draco International. I was a receptionist at the time."

"So you know Mr. Granger?"

"No. This was about ten years ago. He was after my time." She squeezed his arm. "I like you, Edgar, and I know DI can be a stressful place to work. At Goodrich Scents, we strive for a relaxed and happy work environment. Our employees are encouraged to bring their pets to work. We have an animal day care, as well as one for children, right in the building."

It sounded like heaven, but Edgar was committed to working for Mr. Granger. He rather liked the persnickety man and his drunken kisses. And that amazing tongue. "Thanks," he said. "But I'm happy where I am."

The next day, he reported the responses to Mr. Granger.

"Though they accepted, Mr. Tafari, Mr. Dionicio, Mr. Lowry, and Mr. Kaysar declined the offer to bring a date. Ms. Goodrich is bringing her wife. I'm still waiting to hear back about the others."

Mr. Granger leaned back in his padded black leather chair behind his equally official-looking desk. His gaze settled on Edgar. "The Gettys, the Hernandezes, and the Yousifs have let me know they're coming. We'll have a full crew. Get the steaks from the butcher on Sixth Avenue. He always comes up with excellent cuts. Have you found a caterer?"

"Yes. I hired a couple of the cooks from the restaurant here, and I was planning to see if a couple of the servers who had the night off wanted to work for some extra cash. I also ordered these really great chocolates for the gift bags."

Mr. Granger rubbed his chin, and he narrowed his eyes. "Gift bags?"

It hadn't taken Edgar long to learn Mr. Granger rarely got angry. Though he appeared fierce, he was actually very even-keeled. The narrowed eyes denoted confusion, not ire. "Little treats for people to take home as a memento of their lovely evening."

"Okay." He nodded, a sign of thinking and processing. "I've never done that before."

"Change is good," Edgar said. "And since half of your guests are people you do business with, you can never have too much good will.

"Sure. Sounds great. Get a cleaning staff in there on Friday."

"Absolutely, Mr. Granger. I'll make sure everything runs smoothly.

Amar

"Edgar, come here." Amar buzzed the intercom in his phone that went directly to Edgar's desk. In the few weeks he'd been there, his assistant hadn't figured out how to reply back, which meant Amar never knew if he was talking to air until the door opened.

More often than not, Edgar was there. He seemed to have an uncanny knack for knowing when Amar would need him.

He waited for the door to open, but nothing happened, so he buzzed Kimbra. "Where is Edgar?"

"He went out to lunch, Mr. Granger. I'm not sure when he'll be back."

Amar checked the time. It was well past lunch, and he couldn't imagine Edgar taking comp time right now. "Get him on the phone."

"Yes, Mr. Granger."

A minute later, Kimbra let him know Edgar was on line three. He picked up the phone. "Where are you?"

"Your apartment."

Unbidden, an image came to mind—of a semi-naked Edgar laying on Amar's bed, watching with those bedroom eyes as Amar feasted on

Edgar's cock. He shook it away, and when he spoke again, his voice was a little rough. "Why?"

"Um, Mr. Granger, please don't tell me you forgot about the dinner party tonight? You have twelve people coming over for boring business conversation and roasted duck."

Amar could have sworn that he'd requested steak—rare. However, he'd also left the decision-making details in Edgar's hands. For the first time, he was blessedly free of having to be involved with the details of a dinner party. He loved the idea of giving the order and showing up for the result, and the task had made Edgar blossom. Making reservations and arranging for deliveries made him laugh and smile. Overhearing some of the conversations, Amar had no doubt Edgar had charmed every single person he'd talked with to coordinate plans.

"It's not boring," he bristled.

"Mr. Granger, I'm going to sneak something that's actually fun into your schedule one day, and you're going to be amazed at what 'not boring' looks like." Edgar followed up with a laugh that brought to mind visions of kissing him breathless.

He let the comment pass. "Is everything okay?

"Everything is perfect. I'm just overseeing the setup. Why? What's wrong?"

"I was going to send you out for coffee."

"And one of those blueberry crumble muffins?" Edgar chuckled again. "Can I read your mind or what?"

He'd read Amar's mind perfectly, but he wasn't in a position to deliver the goods.

"Mr. Granger, normally I'd have it delivered to you, but today I don't want you to spoil your dinner. This meal is going to be epic, and I need you to bring your appetite."

Amar always had an appetite, but he ceded to Edgar's wishes. "I'll be home in a couple of hours."

He arrived home on time for once. An unfamiliar sense of eagerness overtook him, and he found himself shutting off his computer and hurrying out of Draco International headquarters for the first time in his life. Even Kimbra was surprised to see him go.

Once he got home, he noticed a rather large change. His front door opened to a foyer that led to a spacious living room. Behind the living room was a dining room where he had an elegant and sturdy walnut table. Hand-carved and shipped from North Carolina, it was one of his prized possessions. He loved the table that was large enough to seat fourteen comfortably. Even without the leafs in it, the massive piece of furniture had a presence.

It was gone.

In its place was a round table that looked as if it was made of stone. He crept closer, hoping his eyes deceived him. Stone that massive would ruin his floors. It was suitable for out-of-doors, perhaps.

He ran a finger along the surface to find it smooth and warm. Wood.

"You like it?"

Standing in the doorway leading to the kitchen, Edgar sported a smug smile.

Amar straightened. "I don't see the need."

"It's part of the theme." Edgar rolled his eyes and came closer. He took Amar's briefcase. "You have time for a soak in the tub if you want. I set out some bubble bath."

Bubble bath? Grown men did not take bubble baths. They showered—quickly, even when masturbation was involved.

Before that idea could sidetrack Amar, he took in the entirety of the room. Rich tapestries hung from the walls, obscuring much of his art collection. A suit of armor presided over the table. The candy dishes scattered throughout the room looked like replicas of the Holy Grail, only they were filled with various treats instead of eternal life.

"Edgar, explain what is going on here."

He frowned, which made him appear entirely too sad. Amar fought the urge to take him in his arms and smooth away the confusion.

"Mr. Granger, did you not read the invitation? I gave it to you for final approval."

Closing his eyes, he struggled to recall. He'd thought Edgar wanted him to approve the printing cost. "Refresh my memory."

"Modern Knights. Like King Arthur and the Knights of the Round Table, only today instead of in olden times." Edgar's grin returned, as did the gleam of excitement in his eyes. "You're King Arthur. I know Mr. Kaysar thinks he is, but it's your house, so you get to be the king."

It didn't ring a bell, but Edgar bringing the proof to him for approval did. His attractive assistant had entered the room, merriment sparkling from his eyes and a grin so wide it was the only thing Amar could focus on. The lengths he was willing to go to just to keep a smile on Edgar's face surprised Amar.

With a sigh, he gestured down the hall to his bedroom. "You'd better not have a suit of armor or chainmail for me to wear."

"You take the fun out of everything." Edgar pouted and turned away.

Again, Amar was seized by the urge to take Edgar in his arms. At work, it was easier to resist Edgar's powerful allure, but seeing Edgar in his home sent his mind in a direction that made his libido difficult to keep under control.

Uncertain as to how to respond in a way that wouldn't alarm Edgar, Amar went to his room to change. There, he found Edgar had laid out a suit. The light blue tie was unfamiliar. He lifted it to find it had a subtle sword pattern threaded in gold. "Damned man thought of everything."

A delicate tide of longing surged through him. If only Edgar was a dragon shifter, then everything would be fine. Amar would be free to act on the tender feelings engendered by the mere fact of Edgar's presence. Edgar's scent was on the clothes he held in his hands, and his dragon purred.

He closed his eyes and inhaled, feeding a primal need. Pretty soon, it wouldn't matter what Edgar was or wasn't. Amar was falling for the human, or maybe he'd fallen for the man the moment he'd brushed a crumb from his cheek. One way or another, he felt a powerful need to have Edgar by his side—and in his bed.

An hour later, his apartment was filled with conversation punctuated by bouts of laughter. This was mostly a business meeting, the kind meant to foster relationships among people in key positions in order to optimize the development and distribution of products.

Jeanne Goodrich of Goodrich Scents held a glass of wine in one hand. She was a formidable woman, tall for a human female, and remarkably self-assured. She had an oval face that was fierce, and yet it softened whenever her gaze landed on her pretty wife. She set her free hand on his arm. "Amaricio, where is that handsome assistant of yours?"

They'd been discussing ways to package the scent Jeanne had developed for diffusers Draco International wanted to use in their new personal product lines. They wanted a signature scent that could be used for everything from hair products to deodorants to air fresheners.

Amar hadn't expected anyone except Zeke to ask about Edgar, and that would be mostly to tease Amar about his attraction to his assistant. He furrowed his brow lightly, confused by the question. "He's overseeing meal preparation."

Ms. Goodrich frowned. "I was hoping to see him. He's such a delightful man. My wife absolutely adores him."

This news did not surprise Amar, though he found himself dealing with twinges of jealousy. No one was supposed to love Edgar more than he did. Love? For fuck's sake—where had that idea come from?

Lust, he could understand. But—love? Absolutely not. He forced a smile. "I'll have him poke his head out."

Tito wasn't going to like that. Part of the reason Amar preferred to have Edgar hiding out in the kitchen was to keep him away from Kaysar. While Amar loved his mentor very much, he wanted to limit the man's exposure to his assistant. The less Tito had occasion to observe Amar's reaction to the submissive male, the better.

He made his way into the kitchen to find Edgar seated at the square island in the center of the kitchen, sipping a glass of wine and watching the kitchen staff work. Rich scents filled the room, but his dragon zeroed in on Edgar's unique fragrance. It rumbled an insistent purr.

Edgar glanced over, and a smile lit his face. "It's almost ready, Mr. Granger. Doesn't it smell scrumptious?"

"Yes." Amar wasn't referring to the roasted duck, but he wasn't going to admit it out loud. "Edgar, Ms. Goodrich would like you to come out and mingle for a few moments."

"Sure." Edgar slid from the high stool, a specially-made seat meant to accommodate the height of an adult dragon.

As he came around the corner of the island, Amar noted that Edgar still wore khakis and a white polo shirt. It suited his personality, but it wasn't appropriate for a dinner party. Amar said nothing. He had plans to address the lacks in Edgar's wardrobe.

At the door to the living room, Amar set his hand on the small of Edgar's back. The smaller man seemed to both straighten up and melt into the touch. The purring Amar's dragon had been doing morphed into longing. He fought the urge to pull Edgar into his arms and bury his face in the curve of his assistant's sexy neck.

Amar needed a distraction, so he started talking. "Make small talk for a few minutes, and then excuse yourself back to your duties."

"Edgar!" Brenna Goodrich, Jeanne's wife, held her arms out to Edgar.

He went to her, returning her show of affection with a kiss on either cheek. "Brenna, you look positively stunning. Jeanne was right about you in that dress."

The woman lit up, an inner glow making her smile widen. It was the first genuine show of emotion Amar had seen from anyone in the room. Before this, everyone had been polite and friendly. Somehow Edgar warmed it with the mere fact of his presence.

Brenna grasped Edgar's hand, and her attention turned to Amar. "Amaricio, you have quite a treasure here. Did Edgar tell you how he got my Jefferson to stop running away from me?"

41

Amar had no idea who Jefferson was. He lifted a brow at Edgar. "He didn't mention it."

"It was nothing," Edgar said. "Her dog got away from her, and I brought him back."

"You're too modest." Brenna let go of Edgar's hand and slipped an arm around his shoulders. She pulled him closer for another hug.

At this perfectly benign display, his dragon growled a protest. Amar struggled to keep it at bay.

Luckily, Brenna didn't seem to notice. "He not only brought Jefferson back, but he trained him to stop running away from me at all. That wasn't the first time my naughty boy got loose. He usually gets pretty far before he stops and waits for me. Ever since then, he stays with me when I walk him."

Jeanne joined them, slinging her arm around Edgar from the other side and kissing his cheek. "I tell her not to walk him in heels, but she doesn't listen."

Jealousy surged, spiking his dragon's temper to the fore. Just as he was about to jerk Edgar from between the women, Zeke's hand clamped onto his shoulder. "Am I hearing this right? Brenna is walking the dog while wearing heels? That's confidence."

The two women laughed. Jeanne shook her head. "Ezekiel, that's what attracted me to Brenna in the first place. She has a flair for doing things her own way. I admire an independent spirit."

Amar avoided staring directly at Edgar. It was becoming more difficult by the second to keep his hands from landing on Edgar and drawing him closer. He flashed a smile, but it felt forced and brittle. "There's nothing like an independent and spirited partner to keep you on your toes."

If Zeke was aware of Amar's struggle, he didn't let on. He turned the conversation to business matters, and Edgar soon excused himself to return to his duties.

After he left, Jeanne gave Amar a hard look. "I'm not going to lie to you, Amaricio—I want to steal your assistant. He's positively delightful, and yet you hide him away in the kitchen."

Amar's dragon leaped to the fore, and it took all his willpower not to shift and tear Jeanne Goodrich's limbs from her body.

Zeke stepped between them, shielding the woman though his back was to Amar. "Edgar is indeed an asset. He goes where he's needed."

Brenna flashed a brilliant smile. "I think what my wife means to say is she wishes she could find an assistant as in tune with her needs as

Edgar is to yours. I'm afraid I rather fall short in my role as the wife of a powerful executive."

Jeanne frowned. "You do not."

"We could both use someone like him to organize our lives," Brenna continued. Her attempts to soothe Amar's temper were working. "Wherever did you find him? When we post that kind of position, we end up with those looking for a way into a management position."

"That's mostly who showed up," Amar admitted. It was one reason Edgar had stood out. The rest had to do with the shifter part of his nature. Dragons were wild creatures, driven by otherworldly instinct. "It was a fluke he got an interview. Perhaps I can loan Edgar to help you look for a compatible assistant? He's pretty good at reading people."

Zeke beamed. "That's a fantastic idea."

Just then, a bell rang, summoning them to the table. Each setting had a name card, and Amar found himself with Jeanne on one side and Tito on the other.

After dinner was served by a waitstaff clad in medieval garb—tunics belted with rope and tights for pants—Tito looked to Amar. "Where are the forks?"

Amar surveyed the table. Only knives and large spoons were laid out. He frowned. It wasn't like Edgar to forget a detail like that.

"During the time of King Arthur, forks weren't a thing." Eli Dionicio spoke from across the table. The roundness made it so that everybody had a clear view of everyone else. "They used knives and spoons." Eli tapped the rectangular plate with a pattern resembling oak. "Glad to see you didn't go the distance, though. Wooden trenchers are impossible to clean."

Tito seemed to accept Eli's explanation, and Amar marveled at the small touches. Edgar was truly a treasure.

On the way out, Edgar made sure that each guest took their parting gift—elegant chocolates crafted into sword and crown shapes. The crowns were even painted gold so they shone in the light.

Amar had thrown many successful dinner parties, but this one felt different. His guests had truly enjoyed themselves. The thematic atmosphere made them feel special, and it reflected in everything they said and did. Even Tito congratulated Amar on his way out.

Standing in his silent apartment, he took a closer look at one of the tapestries. It depicted a dragon breathing fire on a knight's shield. Most people would identify with the knight because he was supposed to be the hero, but Amar knew that half of his guests had not. Those from Draco International were dragon shifters. Amar wondered why humans were so obsessed with killing off dragons. Was it because they were larger and smarter predators?

They'd probably shit their pants if they knew that dragons were alive and well and in control of many large corporations.

"I think the dragon is going to win that one." Edgar's soft voice came from over Amar's shoulder. "It's funny—I always wondered what knights felt they were proving by going out and pissing off a dragon. I'll bet they just wanted to be left alone."

Amar wanted to smile at Edgar's observation, but his dragon's purring had turned to stark desire. It was all he could do not to whirl around, pull the non-dragon into his arms, and kiss him breathless.

"Yes," he managed to choke out. "Are the caterers gone?"

"Yep. Everything is almost exactly the way it was. I left it a little cleaner. The rental place will be by at nine tomorrow morning to pick up the tapestries, table, chairs, and the other stuff. I have all the boxes packed and ready."

The cadence of Edgar's words stroked his need, and the meaning barely penetrated. A low rumble vibrated through Amar's chest. He needed Edgar to leave because he was hanging on by a thread. "You may go now."

Edgar didn't move.

Amar knew this without turning around because he was hyperaware of Edgar's scent. Though he stood several feet away, he could hear his breaths and feel the beat of his heart. "Edgar, I said you could leave."

"Are you mad at me, Mr. Granger? Did I do something wrong?"

Where the fuck had Edgar come up with that idea? "You did fine. It's late. You should go home."

"But, Mr. Granger—"

Amar fisted his hands to keep them from shifting into talons, the better to grab and subdue his prey. "Edgar, do you remember the last time you were here and I had a bit too much to drink?"

He felt Edgar back away. "Yes."

"It's best if you leave now."

"Sure. I'll be back before nine to supervise the removal of the rental property." Edgar's quiet footsteps took him out of the apartment.

The soft click of the latch engaging didn't take the edge off the heat rising in Amar's core. Shifting would relieve some of the pressure. Ripping off his clothes, he tossed them to the floor on his way to the wide slider leading to his balcony. As soon as the night air hit his skin, he shifted. Black as night with a lighter belly, his coloring served to hide him in the night sky.

On the street below, he caught sight of Edgar exiting the building. He crossed the street and turned south. Amar tracked his assistant as he navigated the city streets, walking alone with only the street lamps to light his way.

A light rain fell, and Edgar tucked his head down. There was no way he could watch for danger with his face pointed to the ground. And where was his jacket? Though it was summer, the nights were still cool.

Circling the sky, he followed Edgar for about fifteen minutes. His assistant showed no sign of slowing down. Exactly how far away did he live? Why wasn't he driving this late at night?

Then Amar remembered that Edgar didn't have a car, and the city busses had stopped running for the night.

Fuck.

Edgar had been about to ask for a ride home when Amar had told him to leave.

Nothing got his wayward libido under control like realizing he'd failed to protect someone he cared about. Winging back to his apartment took a minute. Amar shook the water from his hair as he ran to his room. He dried his skin and slid into jeans and a plain white shirt.

It took another five minutes before he found Edgar, still walking in a southerly direction. Driving on the wrong side of the street, he pulled up next to his assistant. "Edgar, get in the car."

Edgar glanced over. Water glistened from his dark hair. He wiped where it streamed into his eyes. "No, thanks."

"That wasn't a request."

Crossing his arms over his chest, Edgar kept moving forward, forcing Amar to inch the car along with him.

"Edgar."

"Mr. Granger, I told you once that I like my job and I need to keep it. That hasn't changed."

Shifting had blunted the edge of Amar's wildness, and seeing the position into which he'd put Edgar had banished the rest of his need. "I'm fine now. I promise. It's raining, Edgar. Let me drive you home."

Edgar got into the car. He shivered, and Amar reflected that he should have brought a towel. He had nothing to offer, so he turned up the heat. He glanced around at the deserted street as he waited for Edgar to offer directions.

Then it occurred to him that Edgar planned to return the next morning. He executed a U-turn. "I'm going to have you drop me at my

45

place. You can take my car home with you and bring it back tomorrow. Park in the underground garage." He tapped a sticker on the window. "This is the designated parking spot."

Edgar stared. "Mr. Granger, people in my neighborhood don't drive cars like this. I'd hate for it to get stolen. It's better if you just drop me off."

"I have insurance."

No response came from the passenger seat. Edgar's pensive expression was pointed at his lap.

Amar realized Edgar would stay up all night worrying if he insisted his assistant take the vehicle. He sighed. "Fine. Where do you live?"

Edgar jerked his thumb over his shoulder. "South side of town."

Following Edgar's directions led to a miniscule, dilapidated house that had seen better days. Siding looked like it was slipping down the outside wall, and the gutters had come away from the house in three places. Uneven concrete stuck up at odd angles and made up the front walk. Flowers lined the path, an incongruous attempt to spruce up shoddy surroundings.

Amar refrained from commenting. "Do you usually take the bus downtown?"

"Or Brielle drives me. It depends. She's at work tonight." He paused with his hand on the handle. "Thanks for the ride. I'm sorry about your seat."

He waved away the concern. "It's just water."

With the flash of an uncertain smile, Edgar got out of the car. He ran across the short patch of grass, avoiding the walk completely, and hopped onto the porch. Seconds later, he was inside.

Visions of Edgar's next moves danced in front of Amar's face. He'd strip out of those wet clothes and get into a hot shower. He'd warm up first, and then he'd lather up with body wash. When he got to his cock, he'd take it in hand.

Amar slammed his head back to banish that vision. He vividly recalled how good Edgar's cock had tasted as he'd orgasmed. His dragon grumbled again. Tomorrow was going to be difficult. Perhaps he would make it a point to be gone when Edgar arrived.

"Be careful with that."

46

Amar opened his eyes. Light streamed around the thick, heavy curtains, lending a soft glow to his darkened room, his predator's eyes sharpened the details. Nobody was in his bedroom. Edgar's voice had drifted down the hall, through his closed door, and it penetrated Amar's slumber. He sat up and looked toward his clock to find that it was after nine.

He'd overslept.

Hurrying in the bathroom, he splashed water on his face, gargled with mouthwash, and threw on the same jeans he'd been wearing to pick up Edgar the night before.

He made it to the living room in time to see Edgar close the door behind the movers taking away the rented table. His original table, a sleek and elegant piece, was back in its usual place, but Amar's eyes were glued to the tight black jogging shorts and moisture-wicking shirt gracing Edgar's body. They left nothing to the imagination.

When he'd returned home, Amar had masturbated with the image of Edgar's naked body in his mind. Being faced with something close to the real thing standing in his apartment was almost too much. Amar groaned.

Edgar whipped around. "Oh, I'm sorry, Mr. Granger. I didn't mean to disturb you."

"It's okay. I needed to get up."

Wiping his hand through the blond patch above his right eye, Edgar nodded. "I just need to get the chairs out of the guest room, and then everything will be back the way it was."

Amar called to Edgar as he disappeared down the hall. "Stick around, will you? My tailor is coming at eleven, and I want to get you fitted for a couple of suits and a tuxedo."

Midway to the guest room, Edgar froze. "Mr. Granger, I'm not a suit or tux kind of guy."

Amar bristled at this. He thought Edgar would look exceptional in a suit. "My assistant needs a suit."

Rather than respond, Edgar set about completing his task. Amar went into the kitchen to check out the leftover situation. He found duck, twice-baked potatoes, and cake. Jackpot.

He served up hefty portions of meat and potatoes, and he popped his plate into the microwave.

Edgar came in when Amar was almost halfway finished with his meal. He sniffed the air, but he didn't comment. "I'm finished, so I'm going to go now."

"Fitting," Amar reminded Edgar between bites. "Are you hungry? There are more leftovers in the fridge."

"Mr. Granger, thank you for thinking of me, but I'm going to have to decline. There's no need for me to have a monkey suit. I'm doing just fine without one."

Amar lifted a brow. "Edgar, as someone who represents me in all sorts of venues, I need to have you dressed to impress. You will stay for a fitting, and you will wear a suit to work."

Perching his hands on his hips, Edgar tossed his head in a saucy move. "If you want me to wear suits to work, you gotta pay me a lot more. I can't afford to be running around and spending all my money on clothes."

Amar let his gaze sweep up and down Edgar's body. Those tight clothes looked new. "Like that jogging suit?"

With the roll of his eyes and a swish of his hips, Edgar huffed. "Clothes I don't like. Suits are stuffy. The people who wear them are repressed and unhappy. I have no desire to be repressed or unhappy."

"I wear suits." Amar wasn't sure whether he should be offended by Edgar's assertion. "I'm neither repressed nor unhappy."

By way of response, Edgar lifted a disbelieving brow. "You're not going to argue with 'stuffy'?"

If he was being honest, Amar couldn't, in good conscience, argue with that description of how he behaved around Edgar. If he let loose, he was liable to find himself naked and taking advantage of his employee. Some might not have scruples about that, but the idea of doing anything to stress Edgar ran counter to Amar's heart. And so he worked to keep control of his urges.

In an attempt to steer the topic back to where he wanted it, he indicated Edgar's jogging outfit. "Did you go running this morning?"

"No, silly. I'm not even sweaty."

No one had ever accused Amaricio Granger of being silly. He tried to nail Edgar with a steely glare, but it seemed to have no effect. "You have time for a run before the fitting. You can shower in the guest bathroom. Eleven o'clock, Edgar. This is not negotiable."

Edgar stuck out his bottom lip in a pout. "On one condition."

Conditions were not in the realm of possibility, and yet Amar's curiosity got the better of him. "What condition?"

"Come for a run with me. It's fun, and you need to get out of the house."

"I don't have time." Amar wasn't against running, but he preferred to fly.

"Are you afraid you can't keep up with me?" Edgar crossed his arms. "Fine—we can walk. Go get changed."

This wasn't the way Amar had pictured his day unfolding, but fifteen minutes later, he found himself jogging alongside Edgar. His assistant chattered on about the weather and a host of other things. People called to Edgar, waving and smiling, throughout the entire jog. Amar knew people tended to gravitate toward Edgar's sunny and outgoing personality, but he hadn't realized how many people liked his assistant.

By contrast, nobody waved to or recognized Amar. It was a humbling experience.

Chapter 6

Edgar

Over the next few months, Edgar fell into a routine with Kimbra and Mr. Granger. Kimbra loved the fact Edgar ran all the errands and dealt with coffee runs and Mr. Granger's dry cleaning. Mr. Granger had come to rely on him to take care of all the things that made his life run smoothly. His clothes were clean, his personal appointments did not conflict with his professional ones, and his dinner parties were the talk of the town.

Edgar spent a lot of time at Mr. Granger's apartment. The chemistry between them was always there, simmering below the surface. Sometimes it leaked out in a look or when their hands accidentally brushed together. He never helped Mr. Granger dress, though he did sometimes lay out his clothing. Mr. Granger was keeping up his end of the bargain, smoldering looks notwithstanding. Since Edgar had always been a follower, he found himself relying on Mr. Granger's strength of will to keep that distance between them.

Edgar hired a cleaning service to come in and clean on Tuesdays. He did most of the shopping. He made sure the doormen were tipped regularly. He was there to sign for deliveries or deal with the repair service when Mr. Granger's washing machine needed to be repaired. With Edgar around, his boss could focus on numbers, which he really seemed to like.

But he didn't have any fun. The man didn't do anything to relax. Edgar wondered how he kept in such fine physical condition when he literally sat behind a desk all day. Going to meetings didn't count as aerobic exercise.

Edgar was determined to prevent Mr. Granger from working himself into an early grave, so with the memory of their one run together in mind, he put on his sweatpants and showed up at Mr. Granger's apartment early one morning.

The sexy man emerged from his bedroom wearing plain boxers. He even lacked exciting underwear. He stopped short upon seeing Edgar in his kitchen.

"Did I know you would be here this morning?" His gaze roved over Edgar's attire, asking a question.

"No, Mr. Granger, but I'm glad to see you haven't put on your suit of armor yet." He set a bag on the counter. "Put these on."

Mr. Granger looked inside, and his frown only deepened as he extracted the items inside—moisture-wicking jogging pants and shirt. They were a more masculine version of Edgar's outfit. "Why would I wear this?"

"Because we're going for a jog."

He shoved the clothes back inside the bag. "I don't care to jog."

"Mr. Granger, I happen to know you don't work out. Aerobic exercise will keep your arteries from clogging up. In ten years, when you don't need a triple bypass, you can thank me."

"Edgar, I appreciate your concern, but I have things to do."

"Mr. Granger, you hired me to take care of your personal life, right?"

"Yes, and you've done a good job with that."

"So you agree. Go get dressed. I had Kimbra push back your meeting this morning so we could go for a run." He considered Mr. Granger's lack of exercise and how he'd reacted to his challenge last time. "Or a walk."

Mr. Granger narrowed his eyes, looking for all the world like a dangerous predator. "You're walking me like you do your sister's dogs."

"Yes, and if you're a good boy, we can stop at the park and play fetch."

Edgar was never sure how long it would take Mr. Granger to realize he was kidding. After a lifetime, a reluctant smile appeared, only to be squelched by Mr. Granger pressing his lips together.

"Fine," he said. "A half hour only."

That's all Edgar had scheduled. He didn't think Mr. Granger had the stamina for more. Last time, he'd only taken the boss man for a mile run, and Mr. Granger's pained expression had not escaped his notice.

The jogging pants, black with two yellow stripes down the slick material, fit like a dream, and the neon yellow shirt hugged Mr. Granger's chest, emphasizing and delineating the large muscles there.

Edgar smiled and grabbed two refillable water bottles. "You should wear bright colors more often. Let's go."

Mr. Granger grumbled, but he followed. Edgar started their run the moment they stepped onto the sidewalk in front of Mr. Granger's building, and he led his boss to a nearby park.

Mr. Granger, who Edgar had learned was only a few years older than him, kept up with the slow pace Edgar set.

"Have you ever been to this park before?" Edgar wasn't sure if his jogging companion could talk while running—he hadn't done much more than grunt last time—but he figured it was better to try to distract his boss from the fact he was getting physical exercise.

"Yes. I often walk through here on my way to the office."

"You walk to the office? I thought you used a Draco International driver." Though Mr. Granger had several cars, he lived two blocks from the office building.

"Sometimes. It depends on the weather. I don't care for the rain or really wet snow."

Around them, summer was in full swing. Robins chirped, woodpeckers pecked, and insects made a cacophony of noises. "So, level with me—how do you stay so fit without working out?"

Mr. Granger threw a wry look at Edgar. "I usually get plenty of exercise. I've just been busy with a new project lately."

Edgar's grin grew. "Then it's a good thing you have me to get you out of the office." They entered a part of the path where trees lined both sides, natural beauty lending a sense of privacy.

A cloud blotted out the sun suddenly. Edgar didn't pay it much mind, but Mr. Granger went on full alert. He stopped running, and he pushed Edgar off the path.

"What are you doing?"

Mr. Granger stepped on the backs of his shoes to get them off, and then he slid out of his shorts. Lastly he threw his shirt toward Edgar. This all happened in the blink of an eye, and if time hadn't somehow seemed to slow down, Edgar would have missed the lightning quick moves.

Then the unbelievable happened. Mr. Granger's body grew scales and changed shape. One moment, he was a ruggedly handsome man in the prime of his life, and the next moment, he was an obsidian, fire-breathing dragon.

His wings flapped, and he lifted to the sky. High-pitched screeches, like the kind an eagle would make, filled the air. Holding onto Mr. Granger's clothes, Edgar stepped out from the shadows and peered at the sky.

That hadn't been a cloud blocking the sun. Another dragon had been swooping down on them. Fear knifed through Edgar, and for the first time in years, he wasn't in control. His fight-or-flight reflex triggered a phenomenon that had only happened a handful of times before Brielle had helped him master the necessary self-control.

Edgar shifted into a Tibetan Terrier. Stuck in a tangle of clothes, he wiggled free and dashed to the path to see where Mr. Granger had gone. His heart beat quickly, threatening to tear out of his chest. He'd grown fond of his sexy boss, and he feared the worst.

Though he couldn't see more than light and shadows—almost as if the dragons were hidden by a fog—he made out the shapes of the two fighting figures, and their terrifying screeches echoed in his ears, though he was certain only he could hear it.

After what seemed like forever, Mr. Granger returned. In a blur of wings and scales, he landed in the woods. Seconds later, he emerged, naked, and snatched up his pants and shirt. He glanced around, his predatory eyes taking stock of the surroundings.

Edgar watched from behind a tree.

His boss was a dragon shifter.

A regular guy who morphed into a fire-breathing, scaly-skinned, black dragon.

A whine escaped.

Mr. Granger's head whipped in his direction. "Edgar?"

Edgar, in canine form, cowered behind a tree. For once he was thankful to be a small dog.

The man in black jogging pants and the bright yellow shirt approached. He spied the pile of clothes Edgar had left behind, and he veered that way. He lifted the shirt to his nose and inhaled. "Edgar? Where are you? It's safe to come out."

Drawn by the power and surety of the man's voice, Edgar peeked out from his hiding spot.

Amar

Ice-breathers tended to be jackasses. As a breed, they found a sudden aerial battle invigorating. They didn't see a problem with picking a fight anywhere and at any time with anyone. Lately, they'd been attacking Draco International dragons as a warning.

Amar had heard the telltale tinkling of ice seconds before the ice-breather had attacked. He'd shoved Edgar out of the way, and then he'd shifted. In the air, he'd recognized Lajos Edison, a competitor who had been trying to steal the secrets to Draco International's new defense tech project.

Once upon a time, he and Lajos had been friends, but when Lajos had chosen to follow in the violent footsteps of his ice-breather tribe, they'd parted ways.

This attack was harassment, nothing more. Lajos hadn't been interested in doing serious damage, just in blowing off steam. This was the first time he'd done anything like that with a human around, which alarmed Amar.

On the ground, he'd used his speedy powers to dress before anyone could spy the clothes he'd left behind, but as he'd looked around, he noticed Edgar was gone.

Lajos wouldn't distract him so another ice-breather could kidnap his assistant, would he? That seemed petty and short-sighted, even for an ice-breather.

"Edgar? Where are you?"

He knelt next to a heap of clothes that looked like the form-fitting outfit Edgar had been wearing. An ice-breather wouldn't take the time to make a human strip before kidnapping them. He lifted the shirt, sniffing to get Edgar's scent in his nose. He'd track him that way.

Movement several feet in the woods caught Amar's attention. He spied a tiny dog watching him. It was alone and trembling with fear. Amar frowned at the thing. Edgar would want to stop to talk to the animal, see if it had tags, and return it to its owner. Amar only wanted to find Edgar.

He approached the dog, noting the creamy brown color and the white patch over one eye—just like Edgar. It had a black nose and black rims around deep chocolate eyes. Those eyes, almost obscured by long hair flopping in front of them, held a wide-eyed wariness that Amar had seen twice before on Edgar.

His heart stopped.

"Edgar?"

The dog's tail wagged even though it hung low instead of curling on his back.

Amar crouched down. "Edgar, it's okay. You're safe." He held out a hand. "Come here."

The dog inched forward. His body trembled, and he looked like any sudden move would send him bolting in the opposite direction.

Never having dealt with canines at all, Amar concentrated on gentling his voice and his demeanor. The dog sniffed his hand for a moment, and then he nudged it on top of his head. Amar petted the animal.

"You had better be Edgar, little one. I'd hate to find out I wasted all this time calming down a stray dog when my assistant is out there in danger. He means a lot to me." He picked up the dog, noting how fragile and light he was. It amazed Amar that he could shift into a creature three times his weight and size, while Edgar could do the opposite.

Edgar snuggled into his chest, and he held the dog until he stopped shaking.

"Edgar, I need you to shift back to human form. It's safe. I promise. I've got your clothes, so you'll be able to get dressed."

He meant to set Edgar down, but the dog shifted, and he found himself holding his naked assistant in his arms.

Amar groaned. This fantasy taunted him all day and haunted his nights. He craved Edgar, but he had to settle for having him nearby in a platonic capacity or not at all.

Edgar wiggled down. He turned away to dress.

The silence weighed on Amar's nerves.

"So...What kind of dog are you?"

Edgar jumped, and then he froze. He had put on his pants, and he held his shirt in his hands. "What kind of dragon are you?"

"Sharp-wing. I fought an ice-breather. They're trying to steal research and development secrets."

Edgar turned slowly, and his gaze wandered over Amar as if taking him in for the first time. "Tibetan Terrier."

He needed to put his freaked-out assistant at ease. Noting how often the tactic worked for Edgar, Amar smiled. "I'd always wondered about the patch of blond you have over your right eye."

Edgar's hand went to the anomaly, and he smoothed it with shaking hands.

"It's okay, Edgar. I know how to keep a secret. It's actually nice to know you're one of us."

He jerked his shirt over his head and jammed his feet into his shoes. "One of you? No. Dragons eat dogs. I don't want to get eaten."

Shocked at the sentiment, Amar squared his shoulders. "I've never eaten a dog in my life."

He smoothed his hair again, and Amar recognized the action as an attempt to self-soothe. He closed the distance and wrapped his arms around Edgar. Amar took over stroking Edgar's hair away from his face. Soon the stroking extended down his back. Edgar shivered in his arms, exhaled a long stream of air, and snuggled into Amar's embrace.

"That's better," Amar murmured. "I'll always protect you and keep you safe."

Edgar peered up at him, and he drowned in those trusting eyes. Before he knew what he was doing, his lips brushed over Edgar's softer ones. With a barely perceptible whimper, Edgar's lips parted, and Amar deepened the kiss.

Things happened inside him. Synapses fired molten messages to one another. His dragon, enraged only a short time ago, rumbled with the intent to mark this omega. Relieved his instincts had been right all along—Edgar was somehow meant to be his—Amar lifted Edgar against him. His hands explored Edgar's svelte figure and gripped his tight ass. Edgar's hands roamed Amar's face, beat tracks through his hair, and caressed his shoulders. He wrapped his legs around Amar's waist, and he ground his pelvis against Amar's stomach.

The urge to strip Edgar naked and show him all the ways their bodies fit together threatened to overwhelm Amar. But the attack left him concerned something had happened at Draco International. They wouldn't go after just him.

He ripped himself away from Edgar, holding the omega at arm's length.

Amar panted, but not because of the exercise. Fighting such a powerful desire was hard work under normal circumstances. "Edgar, we need to get to the office. I have to report this attack." He pulled Edgar to him for a brief follow-up smooch. "We will definitely be discussing this later."

An hour later, Amar sat in Tito Kaysar's office, recounting the incident. He conveniently left out any mention of Edgar shifting. He didn't know why, but some instinct counseled him to keep it quiet. After Amar finished relating his tale, Tito folded his hands and studied the middle distance.

"Koren Tafari was attacked this morning as well."

Koren was an engineer working directly on the project in question. Amar sat forward. "Is he okay?"

"Yes. Ice-wings aren't known for their prowess alone, but it seems they're organizing, and that will present a threat." Tito squeezed the bridge of his nose and sighed. "We need to meet. Someplace private. Eli has a place in the Villa Nevado."

"The Andes?" Amar frowned severely. "Go to the snow-capped mountains to plot how to fend off an attack of ice-breathers?"

"They breathe ice," Tito said. "But they love the desert."

Amar considered this. He didn't see the need to go so far away, but he knew better than to question Tito. Kaysar had a good reason for everything he did. "I'll arrange it for this weekend."

"Friday," Tito amended. "Everyone will fly in on Thursday night."

That left two days to make arrangements. Even Edgar would have a difficult time pulling that off in such a short amount of time. Amar sped back to his office to let Edgar and Kimbra know about their next assignment.

Edgar set to work in a flurry of sticky notes and phone calls. Kimbra got on the computer to rearrange his schedule.

"Can I do anything to help?" Amar was reluctant to leave him, and that kiss played heavily on his mind.

Edgar waved him away. "You take care of the meeting agenda. I'll take care of travel, food, and entertainment."

"We won't need entertainment." Amar took that off Edgar's plate before disappearing into his office. "This is work, not a vacation."

The next day, he found himself on a flight to Chile. His schedule had been impossible for the past twenty-four hours, and so he hadn't been able to sit down and talk to Edgar about what happened during the ice-breather attack.

On the private plane, Edgar sat next to him, bouncing around as he peered out the window.

Amar stopped reading through his notes for the meeting when Edgar's wiggling bumped his laptop to the floor yet again. He closed it up and slid it under his seat. "Is this your first time on a plane?"

He hadn't missed Edgar trying to play it cool through the line at the airport, boarding, and takeoff. Though they were flying on one of Draco International's private jets, and there were plenty of empty seats, he'd directed Edgar to sit next to him.

Edgar settled his butt back into his seat. "Sorry, Mr. Granger. I didn't mean to disturb you."

He reached over and closed his hand around Edgar's wrist. "I asked you a question, puppy."

Edgar froze. "Mr. Granger, please don't call me that."

"How about you call me Amar when we're alone?" Amar dragged a fingertip along the sensitive underside of Edgar's wrist. "I want to talk about what happened on our jog the other morning. We've both been busy, but I haven't forgotten."

His gaze dropped, and he nodded as if he expected the worst. "Sure. Amar. What if I slip up when other people are around?"

He shrugged. "Then they'll figure out you and I have grown closer. It's not a big deal."

"If you say so."

The effusive demeanor he'd come to crave was curiously subdued. He'd expected Edgar to be nervous, but he hadn't expected this complete shutdown of emotion. Amar dived in, hoping he was doing the right thing and his honesty would set Edgar at ease.

He looked into those big brown eyes and let himself drown. "I'm attracted to you, Edgar. If you don't feel the same, please don't feel pressured to say so."

Edgar's gaze slid away.

Amar's heart sank. That last kiss—and the first one—had knocked him on his ass. He'd thought he'd affected Edgar the same way. He withdrew his hand from Edgar's wrist. "Once again, I'm sorry. My actions were out of line. I understand if you want to pursue a different position in the company. I'll give you an excellent reference." He'd offered Edgar the option to sue once before, and he'd declined. Amar understood the idea of taking legal action didn't sit well with Edgar.

"I really like this job." His voice came out small and quiet. "I'm good at it."

"Yes, you are. You're easily the best personal assistant I've ever had." Though he was also the first one, Amar couldn't imagine anyone who anticipated his needs the way Edgar did. He was loyal and observant, energetic and happy. Each of those qualities made Amar fall for him.

Edgar clutched his hands over his heart and heaved a dramatic sigh. "Thanks, Amar. That means so much." He followed up with an eye roll. Then his effervescence fizzled out. "Look, I like you. A lot. I think about that first night—when you got drunk—all the time."

Hope returned. Amar held it in check because he needed to let Edgar have his say.

"But I don't want to risk my job. We finally saved enough for Brielle to enroll in classes at the community college. She's wanted to be a nurse forever. She's so sweet and good, and she's taken care of me all these years. She deserves to have her dream come true." He turned to face Amar. "I'm a hopeless romantic, Amar. I fall hard and fast, and then it ends tragically. Brielle is always there to pick me back up. I'd hate for her to also have to quit nursing school."

Amar followed most of what Edgar was saying, but when he mentioned falling hard and fast, his brain seized on that single idea. "I've never felt this way about anyone, Edgar. It's scary, I know, but we can make it work."

"You're not listening." Edgar set his hand on Amar's arm, and Amar wanted to pull him into his lap. "I can't risk losing my job."

Did he think Amar wasn't serious? "Your job is not at stake."

Edgar squeezed his eyes shut. "But when sex enters the equation, then it jeopardizes everything. I mean, it's good when it's good, and it's not when it's not."

Caving the urge to have Edgar close, Amar picked up the smaller man and slid him onto his lap. He stroked his thumb along Edgar's jaw before fanning his fingers through his hair. "Edgar, I know there are risks—lots of them—but I firmly believe that anything worth having is worth the risk."

With that, he brushed his lips against Edgar's. The canine shifter opened on a moan. Amar slipped his tongue into Edgar's mouth, savoring the taste of his lover's kiss. Unlike in the aftermath of danger, passion built slowly. Amar took his time. He caressed Edgar over his clothes, stroking his shoulders, arms, and chest before venturing lower. He slid his palm along Edgar's thigh, an unhurried touch.

Amar's cock stirred, and Edgar shifted his weight. The light brush of his thigh against Amar's erection elicited a groan from Amar's depths. He broke the endless, drugging kiss, and he pressed his forehead to Edgar's. "Tell me to stop, and I will. Tell me to leave you alone, and I will." He drew back and locked his gaze with Edgar's. "Or ask me to make love to you, and I will."

He'd never seen a man look so vulnerable, and the expression tore at him.

"Edgar, I promise to do right by you, no matter what. I want to take a chance on us, but if you don't..." He left the rest unsaid because he couldn't bear to utter ominous words.

Edgar grasped Amar's head on each side, framing his face with his hands. "Make love to me, Amar. I want—I need—to feel you inside me."

His plaintive tone obliterated the last of Amar's control. He pressed Edgar back, laying him across the large, plush seats and settling his weight on top of his lover. Then he captured his mouth for a plundering kiss that demanded all of Edgar's secrets.

Edgar tugged at Amar's shirt, untucking it from his slacks. Amar knelt up and loosened his tie while Edgar unbuttoned his shirt. Working together, they bared Amar's chest. With a gasp, Edgar's hands and mouth were all over Amar's skin, trailing a riot of sensation in their wake.

Small flicks of Edgar's tongue moved lower, and Edgar tugged at Amar's pants. Then his hands were under the waistband and pushing Amar's pants out of the way to expose his engorged cock. Wasting no time, Edgar slid down and licked Amar's length while Amar held himself up on his hands and knees

The reality of Edgar's touch and the heat of his tongue was a million times better than imagining it. Amar groaned. "Fuck, yes. That feels so good, Edgar."

Edgar lifted Amar's cock out of the way and sucked on his sac, careful to pull one ball at a time. Amar ran his fingers through Edgar's short hair, petting his shifter lover and luxuriating in the silky feel of his hair.

Seconds later, Edgar wiggled out from under him and pushed Amar back. Edgar slid to the floor. His hand wrapped around the base of Amar's cock, and his mouth slid over the crown. He played, licking the sensitive crown and dipping his tongue into the tip to lick away the precum.

Edgar slid Amar's cock into his mouth, moaning around the thick member as he took it almost three-quarters of the way. Amar was impressed. His cock was thick and long, and if he concentrated, it was ribbed for pleasure.

Through half-closed eyes, he watched Edgar's head bob on his cock. Amar had never witnessed a more erotic sight. Edgar was a beautiful man, inside and out, and that beautiful man wanted him. He was humbled.

He urged Edgar to abandon his cock. The moment his mouth was free, Amar lifted him and kissed him breathless. "You're wearing too many clothes."

Edgar glanced down as if he hadn't noticed he was fully clothed. "Yes, Amar." He lifted his shirt over his head, and then he shed his pants and underwear.

Amar guided Edgar to stand in front of him. He stroked his cock as he took in the vision of naked male perfection. "You are incredibly beautiful, Edgar. I could spend hours looking at you, touching you, making love to you." A grin stretched Amar's lips. "You know what? I'm going to do all those things."

Edgar's gaze traveled over Amar's body, landing on the cock Amar lazily pumped. "We're going to need lube."

"You don't carry that in your messenger bag?"

Edgar's lips parted as he thought. "No. I'll start, though, if this is what airplane rides with you are going to be like."

"Check my bag." Amar motioned to the travel bag he'd brought into the cabin. It sat on the bench seat across from them.

He watched Edgar bend over to rummage through the bag, and he groaned.

"You have a very sexy ass, Edgar Vidal. I'm going to very much enjoy fucking it."

Edgar widened his stance and curved his back, sticking his ass out to taunt Amar. He reached underneath and spread lube over his anus, and then he looked over his shoulder and winked. "Come and get it, big boy." His hand moved between his legs, spreading lube all over his shaft as he masturbated.

Never in his life had a lover teased him during sex. Amar chuckled. He expected no less from Edgar. Rather than leap on his lover, he let the alpha part of his personality take over. "Hands off that cock. It's mine."

Edgar's ministrations stuttered to a halt.

"Good boy. Cup your balls. That's it. Get a good hold and pull them down." Amar watched with satisfaction as Edgar followed orders. "Ease up a bit. Good boy. Now pull them again."

Hisses and moans issued from Edgar, and subsonic whines only heightened the experience.

Rising to his feet, he approached slowly. "Keep doing that." He ran his palm over Edgar's smooth ass. His skin was creamy, just like his coat when he shifted. When he looked closer, he could make out that the hairs on his legs and arms were patterned like his coat when he was a Tibetan Terrier.

Amar's coloration in his human form had nothing to do with his dragon form. Though his complexion was olive, he was a black dragon. When he shifted, his eyes darkened to black as well. His scales were mottled so that from below he appeared like a dark cloud.

He noted these things, filing them away with all the other things he knew about Edgar, and he took the bottle of lubricant from the smaller man. He drizzled it on his palm, and then he massaged it into the tight pink rosette tempting him with its offer. He inserted a finger, and Edgar moaned. Another finger, and he moaned louder.

"Yes, Amar. Make me yours."

"I will, my lover. First I'm going to play with this delicious ass." Amar bent down and licked that rosette. The lubricant had a strawberry flavor that mixed with Edgar's natural musk to create a dizzying feast for the senses.

Amar morphed his tongue, and he licked from hole to sac. He wrapped his long tongue around Edgar's sac, caressing it as only a dragon could.

Edgar gasped and moaned, and his body trembled.

Continuing the assault on his lover's senses, Amar added a third finger, sawing them in and out to prepare Edgar to take his huge cock. The noises coming from Edgar got louder and quieter. Somehow he managed to gasp in a normal wavelength and whine subsonically.

The whine tingled through Amar's body, creating an urgency that would not be denied. At last he couldn't stand it anymore. He gave Edgar's balls one final lick, and he withdrew his fingers from Edgar's ass.

"This might hurt a bit, Edgar. I've lubed you up quite well, but you're so small and I'm very large."

Edgar chuckled. "That sounds like a porn star brag—oh, look at my prodigious dick. I'm going to skewer you with it, tiny twink. You may not walk right for a week."

In retaliation, Amar slapped Edgar's ass.

"Oh, was I bad?" Edgar waggled his hips back and forth. "Are you going to breathe fire?"

"No, but I will fuck you with my great dragon's dick, which is ribbed for your pleasure."

Edgar peeked over his shoulder. "No way."

Amar lined his cock up with Edgar's tight opening. He pressed forward. "Judge for yourself, puppy."

Edgar gasped. His neck and face turned ruddy. His mouth opened, but no sound came out.

Concerned for his lover, Amar paused. He stroked Edgar's back. "Edgar? Am I hurting you too much?"

Edgar's mouth moved. His lips tried to form words.

Amar reversed direction, slowly easing back.

"No!"

He froze.

Great breaths heaved from Edgar's chest. "You feel so fucking, unbelievably good. Please don't stop." He followed up with that subsonic begging whine that drove Amar crazy with passion.

Unable to stop himself, Amar surged forward. He buried his cock in his lover.

Beneath him, Edgar's body quivered. He reached one hand down to stroke his cock.

Amar fought against his instinct and worked his cock in and out slowly. Or, he tried to. Edgar moved his hips, fucking himself on Amar's dick to a faster pace, so Amar obliged. He grasped Edgar's shoulder with one hand, and the other reached under his lover to masturbate him.

The sounds of grunts, moans, and the sweaty slapping of bodies filled the cabin. Fire traveled through Amar's blood, a product of passion and of his dragon nature. His balls drew up, and he slammed all the way inside Edgar's body. With a cry, he came.

Immediately, Edgar's ejaculate spilled over Amar's hand. He milked his lover until both their bodies stopped jerking. Slowly he withdrew from Edgar.

Edgar collapsed on the seat, crushing Amar's bag.

Amar licked Edgar's come from his hand.

"I can clean up," Edgar said. "Give me a minute." Eyes glassy with pleasure, he smiled softly at Amar.

"I want to," Amar said. "I crave the taste of your ejaculate. I could suck your cock every day."

"I wouldn't turn down an offer like that." Edgar chuckled. "Did you know your eyes are slits, like a lizard's? Is that a dragon shifter thing? I didn't think I changed at all. I mean, I've worked really hard to never shift."

Amar frowned. "My eyes—yes, that's a dragon shifter thing. Why do you work hard not to shift?"

Edgar's gaze drifted away. "I've never met another shifter before. I don't know how it all works."

This was unheard-of. Shifters of all breeds had a responsibility to their offspring. "Your parents? Your sister?"

"My parents died when I was five. Brielle and I grew up in foster care."

Amar had no words. Where was his shifter community? They should have seen to his upbringing. But he let those questions alone. As he got to know Edgar and they grew closer, Edgar would confide all the details to him. In the meantime, he needed to see to his lover's wellbeing.

He lifted Edgar, sat down, and held him in his arms.

Chapter 7—Edgar

Edgar had never felt so secure in his life. Being in Amar's arms was a special kind of bliss he'd never dreamed existed. He felt cherished, which was a completely new concept to him.

In Amar, Edgar had a lover who knew his deep, dark secret and who didn't think it was strange. Amar didn't look at Edgar and see a freak. He saw Edgar's kind and caring side, and he prized it. Edgar wanted to take this risk. This had to be what love felt like. His heart swelled with it. He trembled with happiness and the wonder of it all. Never in a million years had Edgar dreamed a man like this could actually have feelings for him.

Brielle would be happy for him.

"So, you don't know anything about your abilities?"

One thing Edgar envied about Amar was his single-minded determination. He knew the first time he saw Amar that he was the kind of man who got things done. That laser focus on a topic also annoyed Edgar. There were a lot of things he didn't want to talk about, and shifting was one of them—but Amar wouldn't let the topic alone.

Edgar peeled himself from the cocoon of Amar's embrace and picked up his clothes. "What's to know? I turn into a knee-high dog when I'm really upset or freaked out. That's not really a superpower."

He went into the washroom and cleaned up, and then he put his clothes on. When he emerged, he found that Amar had used the second restroom on the plane. Flying on a private jet was really cool for a lot of reasons.

Wearing a suit and looking all kinds of handsome, Amar lounged on a bench seat near where they'd had sex. He motioned to the seat across from him, indicating where Edgar should sit.

Like a good dog, he sat. The part of him that wanted to be valued seethed at being treated in such a manner. "Look, I might turn into a dog, but I don't like to be ordered around like one. I'm a person,

Amar." He threw the name into his declaration to make sure Amar was there as his lover, not his boss.

"I'd apologize, but I'm not sorry. I think you've figured out by now I'm an alpha. It's in my nature to take the lead. That means I tend to give orders instead of make requests."

That description was in line with Mr. Granger's behavior in general. Edgar pulled his feet into the seat and folded his legs under him. "I'll give you that."

"And you're an omega, a submissive shifter. It's one of the reasons we work so well together, Edgar. I need you to be you, and you need me to be me." Amar handed a bottle of water across the space between them. "Don't fight your true nature. You will lose the battle and be miserable in the process. Embrace it, and you will find happiness."

Edgar liked to please people, but that path always led to disillusionment and disappointment. Brielle would understand. A man who'd been born into wealth and privilege would not, so he didn't contradict Amar's assertion. He accepted the water, and he bought time by drinking it.

"Tell me about the first time you shifted."

An order. It wasn't different from how Amar always spoke to him—to everyone, really. But he'd expected to be treated more like an equal after what they'd shared. He huffed.

"Don't be like that," Amar cajoled. "You seem to know nothing about yourself as a shifter. Let me help fill in the blanks."

Edgar considered the offer for a hot second. "You're a dragon shifter. You don't know anything about suddenly finding yourself with dog breath."

"Tell me about the first time you shifted." Amar, it seemed, was not going to be put off.

With a graceless grunt, Edgar gave in. "I was fifteen, auditioning for a musical in the high school near the group home. I'm in the auditorium, and there are about fifty or so kids in there, including Carter Abrams, the boy I'd had a full-out crush on for the better part of the year. So I'm singing, and I hit a high note, and my voice cracks. It's not a little stutter—it's a huge vase shattering on the floor. Even the pianist stopped playing. It was bad. The whole place busts out laughing, even Carter."

The whole time, Edgar avoided looking at Amar. He hadn't wanted to share the incident in the first place, and he didn't want to see pity on his lover's face in the second place.

With a deep breath, he finished the story. "I ran out of there, through the door at the back of the stage. I ran and ran, looking for Brielle."

The muffled sound of the jet's engines weren't enough to fill the silence. Amar gestured for him to continue. "And?"

"And nothing. I was a dog." Edgar rolled his eyes. "It's a good thing she likes dogs. Can you imagine? This strange dog runs up to you, barking its head off because he doesn't know he's a dog and he thinks he's spilling his tale of woe?"

He pictured it in his head, remembering with crystal clarity the mortification coupled with the frustration of Brielle's reaction. She'd called him cute, and she'd thrown him a bite of her snack.

Amar propped his hand under his chin. "Were you more upset about the audition or the shifting?"

"Both. I mean, first the audition, and then the shifting. Brielle picked me up and went around trying to find my owner." The heat of remembered mortification crept up his neck. "I shifted back, and she suddenly found herself holding my skinny, naked ass under her arm. That's when she screamed."

Soft laughter came from Amar.

Edgar scowled.

"Sorry. The image in my head is quite amusing. What happened next?"

"Next?"

"Yes, next. You figured out you were a shifter. What did you do next?"

"Nothing. Brielle figured out it was triggered by extreme trauma, and we worked on techniques to help me when I get upset. It's a good thing I'm so laid-back." Edgar had always been affable and frequently in a good mood.

"Does Brielle shift?"

Edgar shook his head.

"She's not related by blood?"

When people asked too many questions about his family, it put Edgar on edge. He pressed his lips together. "She's my family."

"I know, but—never mind." Amar waved the topic away, making it disappear like a magician. "So you learned to control your shifting abilities?"

"I wouldn't say that. I mean, I shifted the other day when we were attacked by a dragon." If that wasn't a good reason to lose his shit, Edgar didn't know what would be.

Amar frowned. "Can you shift right now?"

Not even Brielle talked about his problem with this much candor. The pair of them had agreed to keep his dirty little secret under wraps. The last thing they needed was for social media to feature a video of him and conspiracy nuts pointing out how it's a fake video. Instead of answering, Edgar shot back. "Can *you* shift right now?"

"You don't have to be defensive with me, Edgar. I'm not judging you. I'm seeking to understand so I can help you." Amar stood up and began taking off his clothes.

While Edgar had loved the sex so far, their conversation had not put him in the mood for more. "What are you doing?"

"I'm going to shift, Edgar. It seems you are either afraid of your true nature or you don't understand it. It's quite clear you have not mastered control of your animal." As he spoke, he peeled out of his clothes. Cords and ropes of defined muscles were revealed. Amar hadn't meant his striptease to be arousing, but Edgar's body didn't get that message. His cock stirred.

To fight the growing evidence of his desire, Edgar busied himself with looking at the details. He noticed small scars dotting Amar's skin, light badges commemorating life events. He wanted to ask about them, but he reasoned now wasn't the time.

In an instant, the man was gone. A large dragon had taken his place. Long and sleek, it filled the cabin. With silent wonder, Edgar looked at the man who'd been his boss for three whole months and his lover for an hour.

Black scales absorbed most of the available light. Where the man had been rugged and muscular, the dragon was tough and strong. Like Amar, the dragon had a long torso. It stretched down the aisle and spilled over onto the seats. His tail curled at the other end of the cabin, looping around because it was almost as long as the rest of his body. The front legs ended in talons with long, curving claws. He couldn't see the back legs, but he assumed they had equally formidable weapons.

His gaze kept returning to the face. The shape was different, like a bigger version of that lizard that puffed out and ran really fast through the desert. The snout was covered with small scales. These increased in size and thickness as they progressed to the back of his head.

"Can I touch you?"

"Yes." Amar's voice seemed to come from between Edgar's ears, which was a strange sensation.

"You can talk?"

"Communicate. Just with shifters." He inched closer, inclining his nose down in an invitation.

Edgar reached out tentatively, his hand advancing until it came into contact with the cold scales on Amar's nose. Then he reasoned it was weird to touch someone's nose. He'd hate if anyone did that to him. So he reached back to stroke Amar's cheek. The scales were cold and hard, a protective armor.

"You probably can't feel this," Edgar said. "I could scratch your belly."

He crouched down, looking to see if there was a way to access Amar's stomach, and then he remembered what Amar had said about his dragon dick being ribbed for pleasure. He tried for a peek, but he couldn't see anything.

In a blink, Amar was back in human form. Edgar found himself facing the exact item he'd been seeking. Instead of making a fool of himself, he stood up.

"My whole body is covered with thick scales. I feel the pressure of your touch, nothing more."

"That has to suck when you've got an itch."

Amar lifted a hand. "Did you not see my talons?"

"It explains what happened to my shirt when I took you home that first night."

With a grin, Amar morphed his hand to a dragon's claw. "I was careful. I'd never hurt you, Edgar."

Thinking about the power imbalance, Edgar realized he'd never be as strong or formidable as Amar. The man he was falling for would never look at him and see a life partner. He was a pet, a responsibility. "I guess we'll never be equals."

Amar shifted his hand back, and a frown marred his rugged face. "Equals?"

"Yeah, like you're my boss, and I'm your subordinate. Usually when people are in a relationship, they're equals, but I can see you're always going to be more than me."

With one step, Amar negated the distance between them. One hand cupped Edgar's cheek, and the other rested on Edgar's hip. "Darling, I don't want an equal. I want a complement."

Crossing his arms, Edgar affected a pout. "You already know you look good naked."

"No—complement with an *e*, not an *i*. You're my other half. You're everything I'm not." Amar's hand slid back, gripping Edgar more insistently. "I love you, Edgar Vidal. You complete me. You make me a better man, and I wish to do the same for you."

When he phrased it like that, their relationship sounded perfect.

"Oh." Heat traveled up Edgar's neck as he realized Amar had just declared his love. All the mushy feelings from before came rushing back tenfold. His heart welled with unfamiliar emotions. "I think I might love you too."

Their kiss lacked heat, but it communicated so much more than arousal ever could.

Amar broke away. "It's your turn."

Edgar had already reciprocated the declaration of love. Mostly. "My turn?"

"To shift."

"I only shift when I'm really afraid."

"In the past, emotional trauma triggered your shifting instinct. Now it's time to learn to control it. You will learn to shift at will, and then we can work on partial shifting." Amar dressed once again.

Edgar helped with his tie. "I'm not sure shifting is a useful skill for me. It's not like I turn into a Great Dane or a Rottweiler. I'm a lap dog."

A satisfied half-smile formed on Amar's lips. "I like having you on my lap, puppy."

"Amar, don't call me that."

"Why? Because you're ashamed of your essential nature? No, I refuse to indulge you in that. You're mine, and I reserve the right to call you by a term of endearment that speaks to the heart of who you are." He resumed his seat. "Now, strip out of your clothes, and shift."

The truth of what Amar said penetrated, and Edgar realized he was ashamed of the fact he turned into a dog. He'd spent his life running from his uniqueness and hiding his true self.

Brielle would understand his decision to break from what they'd been doing.

He concentrated on becoming a Tibetan Terrier, but nothing happened. He opened his eyes to find Amar watching him.

"Keep your eyes open," Amar said. "You want to tap into the most basic part of your nature. Embrace your canine self. Feel it in your heart."

Edgar searched for those things, but he really didn't know what Amar was talking about.

Amar sat forward. "You're hardworking, loyal, and intuitive. You're generous and thoughtful. Own it."

Those were his best qualities, and they also happened to be why people loved dogs so much. It explained why he and Brielle had such a tight bond—she was definitely a dog person. As he thought about who he was, he took pride in all of his best traits. The next thing he knew, he was looking up at Amar—way up. He shook off the clothes that hadn't fallen away when he'd changed form.

A huge grin split Amar's face, and happiness flowed from him and into Edgar. It was energy, and it fed a place deep inside that was starved for acceptance.

Amar petted him, stroking his head and scratching behind Edgar's ears. Before he knew what he was doing, Edgar flopped onto his back and presented his belly to Amar, who obliged by rubbing it.

While that was going on, Edgar concentrated on shifting to his human form. Instantly, Amar's hand went from rubbing his dog belly to stroking his stomach. Edgar's cock woke up fully.

Amar chuckled. "Well, I suppose you've earned a reward." He bent down, and his mouth closed around Edgar's cock.

Edgar hadn't expected that. His lover's lips clamped down, and Amar's tongue cradled his cock. With one hand, Amar cupped Edgar's sac. He fondled and stroked while his mouth worked the entire length of Edgar's shaft.

Lost in the throes of bliss, Edgar touched Amar's head, running his fingers through the alpha's hair and clutching at his shoulder. He thrust his hips, and Amar increased suction. It hurt a bit, but the feeling quickly morphed to pleasure. Heat spiked through his body, an impossible monument he couldn't help but scale.

An orgasm detonated in the base of his spine, radiating through his body, and he came in Amar's mouth. Amar only sucked harder, and his throat undulated as he greedily drank evidence of Edgar's climax.

He lifted his mouth away and smacked his lips. "You taste so fucking good, Edgar. I've been craving this since that first night. If you knew the number of times I wanted to order you to drop your pants and lay on my desk so I could suck you off, you'd be amazed."

Edgar was mostly amazed because the dominant types he'd been with in the past had been more into receiving than giving. His chest heaved with the aftereffects, and his vocal cords weren't ready to move.

Amar pulled Edgar until he sat up, and then he ravaged his mouth with a deep kiss. "You did very well, Edgar. I want you to shift every time you take off your clothes. Practice until you can do it with barely a thought. The more you do it, the easier it will become."

"Well, if I'm going to get rewarded like this, then I'll definitely be practicing. Goodness, Amar—you have an amazing mouth."

Amar grinned. "Puppy, I'm amazing all over."

When Amar had said his friend Eli had a hunting lodge in the Andes, Edgar had imagined an elegant but small wooden structure in the middle of nowhere. Eli Dionicio was an executive at Draco International, meaning he was as rich as Midas, which meant he had nice things, and he was probably a dragon shifter. In the back of Edgar's mind, he figured a hunting lodge was a generous term for "where we bring back the moose we swooped down and killed like an eagle eats a rabbit."

It turned out the structure had more in common with a Swiss chalet in the middle of nowhere. Edgar couldn't imagine a giant dragon swooping out of the sky to drop a moose on the massive deck surrounding the house on all sides. Also, it turned out there were no moose in South America. They had a red stag, which was a really fucking big deer, so Edgar guessed maybe they'd hunt for that. The more he thought about it, the easier it was to picture a deer dropping from the sky.

"Edgar? Are you okay?" Amar's question pulled Edgar from the scatter plot of his thoughts.

"It's really big." The roof sloped at a sharp angle, and the lodge rose three stories high. Light blazed from every window in the place. "Why are all the lights on?"

"The staff is preparing for the guests." Amar slung an arm around Edgar as they waited for the driver who'd picked them up from the airport to unload their luggage.

Edgar took in the backdrop. Snow-capped mountains surrounded them on all sides. Uninvited guests would definitely stand out in this isolated location. "It's beautiful."

And cold. At home, it was the middle of summer. Here they were in the midst of winter. He moved closer to the warmth of his lover.

He angled his head to whisper to Amar. "Can you start a fire with your breath?"

Amar's hand landed on Edgar's ass. He squeezed. "Yes. Then, when my mouth is hot from breathing fire, I'll suck your cock."

Edgar shivered. "Does the staff know you and everyone—you know."

"Everyone here is a shifter of some sort. You'll find alpacas, vicunas, chinchillas, and llamas. I don't know who shifts into what, only that they're not dragons."

"Because dragons are too good to clean toilets?" While Edgar's attitude had warmed at being a *complement* to Amar, he still wanted to be considered good enough to be with Amar.

Laughing, Amar guided Edgar inside. "We're too temperamental and not at all suited to domestic matters. A dragon on the staff would have burned this place down by now. Feline shifters are also not suited for many kinds of work. Like dragons, they're primarily predators. Huemul shifters—Andean deer—built this place."

Edgar had suspected there were more types of shifters in existence. There had to be more than dragons and dogs. "Does every animal have shifters?"

"I would expect so. I've encountered a lot of different types of shifters, especially in regions where humans haven't encroached. But you're the first canine shifter I've come across."

Edgar considered that one. "Werewolves?" On one hand, he found the idea fascinating, but only if he never encountered one. Of course, a week ago, he felt the same way about dragons.

"They keep to themselves, and I hear they're less domesticated than both dragons and feline shifters." He trailed off as they came to the door to the house.

"Mr. Granger, welcome to Villa Nevado. I am Fernando. As you can see, we are still somewhat unprepared, and so I will apologize." Fernando, who had far-set eyes that seemed hyperaware of his surroundings, greeted them. His lips kept puckering as if he might spit, but thankfully he didn't follow through.

Keeping a hand on Edgar's lower back, Amar reached to shake Fernando's hand. "We're early to make sure everything is prepared for when the rest of the guests arrive tomorrow." He motioned to Edgar. "This is my assistant, Edgar Vidal."

Fernando's smile brightened. "Mr. Vidal, of course, we spoke on the phone." He took Edgar's hands between his and squeezed them warmly. "I will show you to your rooms."

He led them up two flights of stairs to a large room that faced north. "This is for Mr. Granger." He pointed across the hall. "That is for Mr. Vidal." As he named the rooms, servants placed luggage in the appropriate spots.

Amar held up a hand. "Put Mr. Vidal's things in my room."

Edgar leaned closer to Amar. "Are you sure that's a wise idea? We're here for work."

"I want you near me, puppy. This is not open for discussion."

Chapter 8—Amar

The open suitcase on the bed held many items, some of which Amar had not packed. He lifted out a thick pair of pants. "Edgar? Are these yours?"

Even though they were too long to belong to the omega, the idea of Edgar packing his things in Amar's luggage made warm feelings flood Amar's insides. He hadn't been looking for love. He'd been immersed in doing his job, and love had fallen into his lap. A soft smile curved his mouth.

Edgar emerged from the washroom and looked at the item Amar held up. "Those are yours. You didn't have snow pants, so I bought some for you."

"Why would I need snow pants?" If he went outside, he'd most likely shift, and dragons could withstand extreme temperatures.

"For skiing. I got you thermal pants, but when I checked the wind chill here, I thought I'd err on the side of caution. I'd hate for you to get frostbite." Flashing a damned cute grin, Edgar snagged the garment bag with Amar's suits and hung them in the closet.

"I'm not going to ski." He stared at the items in this bag, wondering if he should take them out or leave the suitcase open in the corner of the room for easy access.

"You can't come all the way to the Andes in peak ski season and not ski."

This was a great time to disclose one of his failings. "I never learned to ski."

Edgar clasped his hands to his heart and mimed a heart attack.

"You *think* you're funny. I don't need to ski. I can fly."

Picking himself off the floor, Edgar huffed. "I can bark and piss on your leg, but I didn't let that stop me from learning to ski."

One of the things Amar loved about Edgar was the fact he said things that would never in a million years occur to Amar. "I'm glad to see you're embracing your canine side."

"Let me teach you to ski."

"No time. I need to make sure everything is ready to go for dinner tomorrow."

Edgar sat on the corner of the bed, bouncing up and down. "I talked with Fernando. They have it under control. Let's go skiing."

A glance out the window showed the sun setting. "It'll be dark soon."

"Sounds like a yes to me." Edgar hopped up. He threw items of clothing at Amar. "Put these on." Then Edgar ran out of the room. "Fernando—are the skis waxed?"

"Mr. Vidal, the skis are indeed waxed and ready to go. Will you be night skiing at Vista? I can have the car brought around."

"I thought we'd mess around behind the house. Mr. Granger is new to the sport."

At least Edgar didn't intend to make a big deal out of this whole thing. Amar donned the athletic clothing. Twenty minutes later, he found himself on the gently sloping yard behind the lodge.

Edgar motioned to the skis. "Make a V to slow down."

"That's great. How do I get started?"

"Gravity." Edgar pushed him in the back. Amar slid forward several feet before grinding to a halt.

He looked over his shoulder to find Edgar pushing off, which propelled him forward.

"Oh—I'm remembering now. It's like roller skating." Edgar followed his observation with a laugh.

It struck Amar that Edgar probably wasn't an expert skier. Growing up the way he had, Edgar wouldn't have been able to afford lift tickets or equipment. "Edgar, are you sure you remember how to ski?" He didn't want to call him out and chance humiliating his sensitive lover.

Edgar stopped next to him. "I taught ski lessons one season, but it was for downhill skiing. This is more like cross-country. I wanted to take it easy your first time. You know—with you being a virgin snow bunny and all."

"Snow bunny? I'll show you a snow bunny." Amar reached down and scooped up an armload of white powder. He tossed the entire load at Edgar. It wasn't great for packing, but it was perfect for playing.

With a screech, Edgar lurched forward. "Amaricio Granger, revenge is a dish best served cold." He slid around, proving he did, in fact, know some ski moves, and he tossed a ball of snow at Amar. It shattered on impact, spraying powder everywhere.

Amar leaped, landing on top of Edgar. They slid and rolled downhill, making a lot more progress on their backs than on skis. Amar managed to get a handful of snow down Edgar's shirt.

The dog shifter let loose with a soulful howl of surprise, but he retaliated by shoveling snow down the back of Amar's pants. The pair wrestled playfully until they were both soaking wet and panting.

Amar collapsed on his back in the softness of the snow. Despite their joyful noises, silence blanketed the area. "I can't remember the last time I had this much fun."

Edgar rolled on top of him. "Learning to ski was a good idea."

He wasn't sure he'd learned anything about skiing, but he had learned other things—namely that Edgar had a really fun side. Since Amar lacked one of those, he doubly appreciated the playfulness Edgar brought to his life.

Peering deep into Edgar's eyes, he made a decision. This was the man with whom he wanted to spend the rest of his life. As soon as they returned home, he was going to arrange for a romantic proposal.

He wrapped his arms around Edgar and his many layers of wet clothing. "I love you."

Edgar pressed his lips to Amar's. "Let's go inside. We can make out in the hot tub and then have mad, passionate sex in your bed."

"I like that plan." Amar got to his feet and lifted Edgar to his. "What happened to our skis?"

Somewhere along the line, they'd lost their skis. Edgar pointed up the hill. "There. We should get those. Fernando might not like me anymore if we become a pain in his ass."

Later he made slow love to Edgar, and then he held him in his arms as they fell asleep.

In the morning, Amar woke to emptiness. Next to him, the bed where Edgar had slept was cold, and no sounds came from the bathroom.

He sat up. "Edgar?"

No response.

A part of him refused to believe Edgar would leave without waking him up first, but as he padded to the washroom for a closer check, the silence said it all. He looked around, but there was no note, no text, and no email to let him know where Edgar had gone.

Amar sat on a chair and closed his eyes. "Get it together, Granger. He's here somewhere." The alpha dragon part of him wanted to tear the place apart until he found his omega, but the rational part of his brain prevailed. Amar had slept late. Edgar was most likely overseeing all the last-minute details to make sure tonight's meetings went off without a hitch.

This irrational need to have his omega within arm's reach was a side effect of his alpha nature. It was a remnant of eons of protective instinct, and the more Amar tried to fight it, the more enraged his dragon became.

There was no other choice but to find Edgar. He dressed quickly and sailed out of the room. Sounds of staff were absent on the third floor. On the second floor, he heard them moving around, preparing the rooms for the expected guests. The main floor bustled with people rushing about. Some dusted and polished. Others moved furniture. One arranged plants and vases of flowers.

Edgar's voice pulled him toward the dining room. He found his lover reading a list of orders to a cluster of staff. "There must be meat with every meal, but it shouldn't be the same. Brisket tonight for dinner. Honey-baked ham with breakfast tomorrow. You can do bacon the day after and sausage the day after that. I know that many of you are vegetarians, but meat is the main protein source for our guests, so do not skimp on the portion size and be prepared to serve seconds."

After several questions, that gaggle of staff moved away and another took their place.

"You're on entertainment detail. We're not going to need a ton because this is a business trip, but even the most serious of businesspersons needs to blow off a little steam. Tonight will have a gambling theme. Rodrigo, have the tables been delivered?"

"*Si*, Senor Edgar."

He clapped his hands. "Great. Get those set up in the great room after their first meeting while dinner service is going on. Then call me so I can supervise testing to make sure everything works."

Amar objected to the idea of Edgar leaving his side during dinner. "Edgar, surely one of the staff can test the tables. There is no need for you to miss a meal."

Edgar turned, a smile lighting his handsome face. "Good morning, Mr. Granger. Thank you for your concern, but I won't miss dinner. I'll just eat a little later."

With the wave of his hand, Amar dismissed the staff. He pulled Edgar to him. The moment their bodies connected, a wave of relief washed over Amar. He leaned down and closed his lips over Edgar's, demanding a kiss. The taste of his omega was ambrosia, but it wasn't enough.

The gentle pressure of Edgar's hands against his chest had him rethinking his urge to deepen the kiss. He broke it. "What's wrong, my love?"

"Mr. Granger, I'm working."

Last night, Edgar had breathed his name passionately. This morning, he was trying to put distance between them. Amar wanted none of it. "Edgar, you will call me by my first name."

"When we're alone. We're not alone."

"All the time." Amar slid his palms from Edgar's shoulders and down his arms until he could take Edgar's hands in his. "I don't care who is around."

Heat stole up Edgar's neck. "Are you sure?"

"Yes. I love you. I wish to shout from the sky that you are mine." He leaned down again. "I missed you this morning. Why didn't you wake me?"

"Because you needed the rest. You've been working nonstop." Edgar's eyes softened dreamily. "I'm not going to lie—it was hard to leave without rubbing myself on you."

Amar suppressed a shiver of desire at the idea of waking up to Edgar's body wiggling on his. "Next time, do it. Don't fight your instincts. Did you shift this morning when you got dressed?"

Edgar's gaze darted away in alarm, searching to see if anyone overheard.

"Puppy, I told you everyone here is a shifter. If you weren't, you'd be the odd one out."

"I didn't have time." Edgar stared at the floor. "Please don't be mad. I didn't want to wake you up."

Without a word, Amar took Edgar by the hand. He led him up two flights of stairs to the room they shared, and he closed the door. "Shift."

"Amar, be reasonable. I have work to do. The driver already left for the airport to collect Mr. Tafari, Mr. Dionicio, Mr. Lowry, and Mr. Kaysar. They'll be here in time for a late lunch, and then you'll all want to get a meeting in before dinner. I know how much you executive types love to meet." His lower lip stuck out in a sexy pout.

By way of response, Amar lifted his brow expectantly.

Edgar grumbled as he took off his clothes. When he'd first come to Amar, he hadn't worn suits. He'd been partial to polo shirts and khakis. That had not changed over time, except that now Edgar owned a few suits and a tuxedo. He'd order Edgar to wear a suit to dinner tonight. He wanted to show off the man of his dreams.

When Edgar was naked, Amar had to work to keep himself in check. His dragon wanted this man with a desire that almost incapacitated Amar. He craved the creamy taste of Edgar's climax, which was new for him. He'd never wanted so badly to suck on an omega's cock before.

Edgar wiggled around, breathing in and out in an effort to follow the protocol Amar had set down the day before. It took a few minutes, but Edgar shifted into his canine form. He ran to Amar, his tail wagging so hard his hindquarters shook.

Amar petted him. "Good job, Edgar. Don't worry about how long it takes to shift. Like I said, the more you do it, the easier it will get." He brushed the long hair from Edgar's eyes. "You need a trim."

Immediately, Edgar shifted back to human form. "Nuh-uh. Brielle trimmed my bangs once, and when I shifted back, it looked like a bad haircut."

"You can't see with all that hair in your eyes."

"I don't plan to be in dog form a lot, so it's pointless to argue over it."

Realizing Edgar still didn't feel comfortable with his canine form, Amar traced his fingertips along Edgar's jaw. "Sometimes it's freeing to spend time in your animal form. One day, I hope you will understand and embrace that. For now, though, you did a good job shifting."

He drew Edgar closer and captured his omega with a searing kiss.

"Amar, I have work to do."

"Keeping me happy is your number one priority." Amar peppered kisses along Edgar's jaw and down his neck. His hands roamed Edgar's soft flesh, and his fingers dug into the solid muscle. He loved how his omega's silky, pliant exterior disguised the strength and resilience underneath.

"Yes, Amar." Edgar's head dropped back to allow Amar better access. His hands remained a flurry of activity as the loosened Amar's tie and unbuttoned his shirt and pants.

A fire raged in his veins, and Edgar's touch both stoked and soothed it. Amar wiggled out of his pants. His shirt hung open, but the urgency of need made him not care. He set Edgar on the edge of the bed. His lover settled onto his back and lifted his legs out of the way.

Amar snagged the lube from the bedside table and drizzled it onto Edgar's anus. He put more into his hand, and he lubricated his cock. "This is going to be quick, Edgar, and you may not climax until I say so."

Edgar lay spread out on the bed, a submissive omega awaiting his alpha's pleasure, and that subsonic whine pulsed from deep in his chest. Amar positioned his cock at Edgar's entrance, and he pressed forward. He did not partially morph to make his dick ribbed. He didn't want Edgar to have an orgasm while he was fucking him.

Edgar's sweet heat enveloped him, welcoming him home with a tight hug. Amar set a frantic pace. Driven by his animal instinct, he pounded into Edgar with swift jabs. Molten heat ignited in his core. This coupling was more intense than anything Amar had experienced in his life. Love for this omega combined with the possessiveness of his dragon. As his orgasm overtook him, Amar threw his head back. Flames accompanied his roar, and he didn't want to singe his lover.

Waves of pleasure rioted through his system. Beneath him, Edgar writhed and shouted, his movements jerky and feverish. His hand pumped his cock.

The erotic sight inflamed Amar's need. He had to taste his omega. Withdrawing from Edgar's body, Amar knelt down. He pushed away Edgar's hand and devoured his lover's cock. He swallowed all of Edgar's long cock, bobbing his head along the length until his omega shouted his orgasm. Hot jets of ejaculate spurted into Amar's mouth, and he greedily swallowed that sweet cream.

Amar sat back, amazed. Every time he came together with Edgar, it was more intense and meaningful. The power of his feelings for this man left him stunned.

After a few minutes, Edgar sat up. He crawled onto the floor where Amar sat, and he straddled the larger man. "Amar, I love you. I've had crushes before, but nothing comes close to what I feel for you. It's huge. Momentous. I'm afraid."

Amar wrapped his arms around his omega. "Don't be afraid, puppy. I vow to love and protect you, to cherish you and care for you." He'd never spoken like that to another before. It seemed like a marriage vow, and yet it was so much more. He trailed kisses along Edgar's shoulder.

When they returned from this trip, he would move Edgar into his apartment.

Tito Kaysar was a larger-than-life character whose opinion carried more weight among members of the Sharp-Winged Tribe than any other. He'd trained Amar as a fighter, and he'd mentored him in the pursuit of his dream of earning a degree in international business. Amar wanted his blessing of his union with Edgar, but he wasn't sure he'd get it. Tito tended to want dragons to marry other dragons.

While Tito's approval, or lack thereof, wouldn't change Amar's mind about Edgar, he wanted it. What's more, he knew his parents would love Edgar. His mother, in particular, had always advocated for Amar to follow his heart.

As Edgar had predicted, once everyone had arrived, they'd eaten a late lunch and immediately began meeting about how to solve the problem with ice-breathers trying to steal the technology Koren was in the process of developing.

Koren Tafari was older than Amar by a decade. He'd been a hotshot researcher when Amar had started at Draco International eight years before, and now he had achieved international acclaim for his innovative designs and application of technology.

The forty-year-old dragon didn't look like one of the top minds in the world. His hair was shaggy and long, and he'd missed more than a couple spots shaving. He had broad shoulders, though his trim build lacked the traditional bulk of most dragon shifters. Even his clothes were sloppy and wrinkled. It was only when one peered closer that they noticed his intense blue eyes.

Koren lounged on a sofa and swirled wine in his glass. Next to him, Zeke presented an opposite image. Always put-together and built like a comic-book hero, Zeke's handsomeness was the first thing people noticed.

Tito sat on a chair like the one Amar occupied.

Their host, Eli Dionicio, closed the door to the sitting room. Of them all, Eli looked like he was the most approachable. His smile was open and friendly. He had the kind of demeanor that invited confidence, which made him perfect for marketing. Eli was also the public face of their company. Whenever anyone had to speak to the press, they sent Eli and his trustworthy face.

"We're alone now. Let's get to the business at hand." Eli perched on the edge of another sofa. "Ice-Breathers have infiltrated Research and Development. The attacks on Koren and Amaricio were a diversion to make us think they were still searching for the tech."

Amar blew out a breath. "Koren, is it finished? Did they get everything?"

"Yes," Koren said. "I was about to start the final stages of testing. If they get it out there first, I'll have blown two years on this."

"In the old days, we would have killed them," Tito said. "We would have battled mightily, and to the victors go the spoils."

Eli winced. "It's not the old days anymore. We all have companies, and the humans have made so many laws and regulations. They would treat it as a high-profile murder, and the Ice-Breathers would not cooperate in covering it up. Why would they? Making us look bad is in their best interest."

"It is confining," Zeke agreed. "I propose that we steal something from them."

Koren made a noncommittal noise.

"You don't like that idea?" Zeke leaned forward. "They steal from us, but you don't like the idea of retaliation?"

"I may have stolen the initial idea from them." Koren rubbed his thigh and took a sip of wine. "I may have had drinks with Lajos Edison, and we may have fooled around. While I was there, I may have seen a notebook where he'd worked out an idea I'd been fiddling with for a few months. He might have made a breakthrough or two before I did."

As Chief Financial Officer, Amar spent his time making the numbers work out. The Sharp-Winged Tribe had been competing with the Ice-Breather Tribe for millennia. He'd employed creative measures a number of times where accounting was concerned, so he wasn't going to pretend outrage at what Koren had done. The Ice-Breathers were like annoying siblings, and their tech was like a stash of candy. They each stole from the other.

Amar tapped his fingertips on the arm of the comfortable leather chair. "We're not going to do nothing, though, right? Otherwise why meet like this?"

Tito cleared his throat. "I'd like to hear your ideas for how to proceed. We've spent millions honing this design. We need to turn a profit."

For the next five hours, they brainstormed ideas. Amar didn't love any of them, but some were better than others. This was definitely going to take the whole weekend. He was glad Edgar was there. After that meeting, he wanted nothing more than to immerse himself in his lover.

The announcement of dinner broke up the meeting. Amar found Edgar in the foyer talking with Fernando. He didn't care about the substance of their conversation. He swooped in and scooped Edgar into his arms, reeling him in for a blistering kiss.

"After dinner, I'm going to take you upstairs and make you come until you pass out." He smacked another kiss on Edgar's lips.

Edgar smiled. "Amar, after dinner, I'm dealing blackjack. I'm running the casino tables."

"Didn't the rental of the machines come with dealers?"

"Not way out in the middle of nowhere. It's okay. I spent a few months working as a blackjack dealer, I'm already good at poker, and I spent the last couple hours learning roulette." He smoothed the lines of Amar's jacket as he explained. "But I promise not to leave the bed in the morning without waking you up."

While Amar sought a way to handle the issue so it would come out in his favor, Tito's booming voice interrupted them.

"Amar—a word?"

Reluctantly, he disengaged from Edgar's embrace. "I'll see you at dinner."

He followed Tito upstairs and into the leader's room.

As soon as the door closed, Tito faced him. "When I was your age, I had an assistant much like Mr. Vidal."

Amar seriously doubted that. If Tito had met anyone like Edgar in his life, he'd be married and blissfully happy instead of thrice-divorced and often surly. "You were in love?"

A dry blast of laughter escaped Tito. "I thought so at the time." He clapped a hand on Amar's shoulder. "Humans aren't meant to mate with shifters. They can't handle our vigorous needs or our possessive nature. Even now, I see Mr. Vidal chafing under the weight of your demands."

"He's not chafing." Amar scowled, rejecting Tito's observations wholesale because Edgar wasn't human. He was a shifter.

"He's delicate. He's trying to balance the responsibilities of being your assistant with your demands as a lover. He looks tired. I'll bet you kept him up late last night, and he rose early this morning to fulfill his duties." Tito arched a single brow, daring Amar to lie.

Amar couldn't. Edgar had dark smudges under his eyes, and his normally energetic demeanor had been subdued in the foyer. He hated that another had to point out he was overtaxing Edgar. The health and wellbeing of his omega was his responsibility. They had only been together for a day, and already Amar was letting him down.

As his omega, Edgar's primary job had nothing to do with being an assistant. He was Amar's complement, and it was time for Edgar to step into that role. With a decisive nod, Amar said, "I will remedy the situation."

Tito smiled. "See that you do." He set a hand on each of Amar's shoulders. "Amaricio, you've always held a special place in my heart."

Amar melted. His mentor meant the world to him as well. "And you in mine."

"I'm going to ask a favor of you. It won't be unpleasant, and it will save the company. Actually, you might like this assignment quite a bit."

Though Amar didn't know the details, he trusted Tito. "Anything."

"Great. We'll discuss the details at dinner."

Chapter 9

Edgar

"After dinner, I insist that you come up here and go to sleep."

Edgar straightened Amar's tie as he listened to instructions. "Can't. Casino night."

"Fernando has found members of the staff willing to work overtime as dealers." Amar framed Edgar's face in his hands. "Puppy, you're exhausted. Let's get you dressed for dinner, and then you'll come up here to sleep."

While he was close to falling over, Edgar chalked it up to not having travel experience. He was used to working long hours, but he'd never before felt so drained. "I already ate."

"What?" Amar's expression darkened. "I told you I expected you to dine with me."

Though Amar wanted him there, Edgar knew he wasn't welcome. The other four alpha dragons wanted no distractions, and Edgar understood he was a distraction for Amar. Even now, Amar was late for dinner because he'd tossed Edgar to the bed and sucked his cock as if it was the secret source of his amazing power.

"Amar, you guys have private matters to discuss, and don't think I didn't see the disapproval on Mr. Kaysar's face this afternoon in the foyer before he hauled you off to his room for a private chat." Edgar smiled gently. "I'll wait for you here, okay?"

With a low growl, Amar gave in. "Fine. Sleep naked. I'll be waking you up when I return."

Edgar grinned. "I can do that."

After a passionate kiss, Amar swept from the room, taking with him every last ounce of Edgar's energy. He sank down on the edge of the bed. Sleep sounded good right now, but he'd promised Amar he would shift every time he undressed. If he slept in his clothes, did that mean he didn't have to shift?

A knock at the door pulled him to his feet. He opened it to find Mr. Kaysar on the other side. Edgar summoned a friendly expression. "Hi, Mr. Kaysar. You just missed Amar. He already went down to dinner."

"Without you?" Mr. Kaysar frowned.

"I figured you guys had business stuff to take care of, so I had dinner separately."

Mr. Kaysar looked down the hall toward the stairs. All was silent. Just when Edgar thought he'd leave, he stepped into the room and closed the door. "Mr. Vidal, I'd like to have a word with you."

His boss's boss wanted to talk to him. This didn't sound good. Edgar swallowed. "Yes?"

"You're a very good assistant."

"Thank you."

"I know you're not going to be with Mr. Granger much longer, but I'd hate for Draco International to lose you. I'd like to offer you a job of your choosing in any of our locations around the world. Have you ever been to Toronto? How about London? Or maybe somewhere a little more exotic?"

Edgar backed away. "I don't understand. What do you mean I won't be with Amar much longer?"

Compassion softened Mr. Kaysar's craggy features. "He didn't tell you. I'm not surprised." He sighed. "Amaricio is getting married. It's all arranged. In light of your former relationship with him, you'll need to be relocated. I'm also arranging a generous bonus for you. Of course, you'll have to sign a nondisclosure agreement. I just didn't want to see your talents go to waste. You're a valuable part of the Draco International family."

This wasn't true. "Amar wouldn't do that to me."

Mr. Kaysar shrugged. "See for yourself. Come downstairs at eight-thirty when the engagement announcement is scheduled." He glanced around. "I'll have Fernando move your things across the hall. Amar's fiancé won't want you here with him."

With that, Mr, Kaysar left.

Edgar sank down onto the edge of the bed, this time in shock. Amar wouldn't do this to him. He'd told Edgar to sleep naked. That wasn't the order of a man who wanted him to move out of a room he'd insisted they share.

In a daze, Edgar crept down the stairs. From the foyer, he could hear the din of conversation in the dining room. They spoke in a

86

mixture of languages, English and what Edgar had found out was a dragon dialect.

The noise level ebbed and flowed as courses were served.

A knock on the door interrupted his spying. Edgar slipped away, taking the stairs two at a time to get out of sight before a member of the staff answered the front door.

Edgar didn't recognize the woman who opened the door, but it didn't matter. Two men came inside, a cold wind blowing through the open portal to usher them inside. They were both tall and broad-shouldered. They had blond hair and festive smiles. Edgar could objectively say that both men were handsome. One was thinner and smaller, and he laughed at something the larger man said.

He exhaled, and frost formed in the air before him.

The servant took their jackets and pointed them toward the dining room. Another man came in with bags, and the servant dispatched two valets to take them upstairs.

A shiver of apprehension ran through Edgar. Not caring if he was seen, he went down the stairs and slipped into the dining room.

No one noticed him.

Mr. Kaysar shook hands with the men. "Gentlemen, I believe you all know Lajos Edison." With the sweep of his arm, he indicated the larger man. "And this is Anshu Bray."

The thinner man bowed with a flourish, and he came up with a flamboyant grin. "It's a pleasure, gentlemen." He winked at Amar. "Amaricio, you're even more handsome than I remember."

Amar didn't appear to have a reaction. His gaze riveted on Mr. Kaysar. "Tito, what's going on here?"

"Peace. A merger. The Ice-Breather Tribe has agreed to combine operations with the Sharp-Winged Tribe." Mr. Kaysar grinned. "Through marriage, we will have peace between us. See? This is so much better than battles and assassinations."

Mr. Lowry lifted a finger. "Tito, who is marrying whom?"

"Amaricio will marry Anshu. They have both already agreed."

Nobody appeared surprised at this announcement. Amar didn't even seem to have a reaction.

Edgar gasped.

Amar's eyes went to him, and his face darkened with fury.

Rather than face the wrath of the man who had betrayed him, Edgar fled. He went to the room and threw his things into his bag.

Was this why Amar had avoided starting a romantic relationship with Edgar for so long? They had chemistry from the start. That first kiss—the inexplicable jealousy—that first blowjob—it all added up.

Amar was attracted to Edgar, but he didn't see him as a life partner—a complement.

Edgar wasn't a dragon, and Anshu was.

He dragged his bag across the hall into the empty room Fernando had offered him only the day before.

A knock sounded at the door, and Mr. Kaysar came inside even though Edgar hadn't invited him. He closed the door and took Edgar's hands in his. "Mr. Vidal, I'm sorry you had to find out like this. I begged Amaricio to tell you himself."

Edgar had nothing to say. His heart crushed under the weight of an incredible sorrow. He wanted to go home and cry to Brielle. "I want to leave," he said.

"Yes, of course. I had the driver pull a car around back. You can slip out that way." Mr. Kaysar lifted Edgar's bag. "I'll have the rest of your things sent to your address."

"Thank you." Edgar wiped tears from his cheeks. He followed Mr. Kaysar down the servants' stairs and out the back way. The moment he stepped into the snowy evening, reality hit him square in the face. The cold air drove away the exhaustion and the emotional malaise that had impeded Edgar's thinking in the first place.

Amar loved him. He'd said so repeatedly even though he didn't have to. He'd been the one pushing for more with Edgar. He'd wanted Edgar at his side when he woke up in the morning and at dinner. The fact Edgar hadn't been at the table was of Edgar's doing.

The fury on Amar's face hadn't been directed at Edgar, but at Mr. Kaysar—the man who'd duped them both. It was likely Amar had been blindsided by the announcement as well.

Edgar came to an abrupt halt.

Mr. Kaysar handed Edgar's bag to the driver, and he faced Edgar expectantly.

Edgar shook his head. "I'm not leaving until I talk to Amar. If he wants me to go, I will."

The way Mr. Kaysar's face hardened said it all. "It's unfortunate you aren't as innocent and simple as you look."

A sharp pain radiated from the back of Edgar's skull, and the world went black.

Amar

Eli and Zeke pinned him against the wall.

"Don't shift," Zeke said. "If you shift, we'll have to shift, and then we'll fight. You'll lose because you can't take us both together. Then Eli will have to remodel this lovely lodge so soon after building it."

Amar was not in the mood for Zeke's humor. His gaze was locked to the place Edgar had been standing. His mind replayed the devastation on his omega's face at Tito's announcement. "Release me."

"I know you want to go after your boy toy, but think for a moment how that would look to your new fiancé who is here primarily to promote peace between our tribes." Zeke threw an elbow to Amar's stomach to stop him from wiggling free. "Sorry, buddy, but you're freaking strong, and I can't let you do something to undermine this deal."

At the explanation, Amar froze. "You were in on this."

Zeke blew out a stream of air. "No, but you have to admit that it's a good idea. You and Anshu are compatible on many levels. You're both in finance. You both like to work a lot and wear fine suits. He's basically the Ice-Breather omega version of you."

Amar nailed Zeke with his most venomous glare. "I don't want to marry myself, you ignorant ass. I love Edgar."

At this, Eli barked a laugh. "A human? Come on, Grange. You know it won't last. This is what's best for us all. You can marry Anshu, and the two of you can raise an army of math geniuses."

Koren had ushered their Ice-Breather guests from the room when Edgar left and Tito followed him, so none of them worried about being overheard.

"He's not human." Amar gritted his teeth. Edgar might not be comfortable sharing his secret, but now was not the time to indulge his sensitivity. "He's a shifter."

"It changes nothing," Eli said. "He's not a dragon."

"Is he a horse?" Zeke chuckled as he voiced the question. "I've seen him in snug pants, and I know he's well hung."

Eli's grip tightened on his arm, but he got the other one free, and he punched Zeke, clipping his former friend on the jaw. A brawl ensued, and at the conclusion, Amar found himself face-down on the floor with two large shifters on top of him.

"I know you're mad right now, but when you calm down, you'll see we're doing this for your own good." Zeke's voice came from over Amar's left ear.

"The fact you would discount my feelings in this matter means we are not friends." Perhaps they'd never truly been friends. Losing Zeke tore at Amar's heart, but he'd rather cut loose a bad friend than lose the man he loved.

The sweep of headlights through the room announced Edgar's departure. Amar roared. Flames shot from his mouth, and he shifted. In a rage, he lifted the dining table and heaved it through the window. Then he took off in pursuit of his lover.

Eli and Zeke were on his tail. They dive-bombed him, knocking him to the ground. The snow-covered, mountainous terrain did not make for a soft landing. They crashed hard, skidding and bouncing over inhospitable and unforgiving bedrock. Jagged peaks tore scales from his body. Red-hot spikes of pain shot through him, but he would not be swayed.

The rough landing had knocked Eli and Zeke off him. Amar rocketed into the sky. Circling high above, he searched for the car. It was not difficult to guess it was headed toward the airport. There was no other way to leave the country.

He followed the road, and he'd just spied the car again when he heard his former friends and tribe-mates coming up on his tail. Whirling, he faced them. Rage and fury fueled his movements, and he fought without mercy.

Tearing and slashing, he roared and shot flames at his adversaries. Eli and Zeke circled him, keeping him contained. A third dragon joined the fight, and Amar recognized Tito.

"Come back to the lodge," Tito called in their ancient language. "Your human paramour has chosen to go home. Hear us out, and if you still wish to pursue him, we will stand aside."

Amar had spent his life looking up to Tito. He'd been impressed with the man's power and authority. He'd even worshipped Tito's ruthless side—until now, when it was turned against him. "There's nothing to discuss. You disregarded my wishes and chased away the man I love. I'll not forgive you for that. Ever."

As one, the trio converged on him. Even before they hit, Amar knew the fight was lost. And yet, he fought until his body gave out and blackness descended over him, forcing him to pause.

He woke in a soft bed. His first thought was he'd ordered Edgar to wake him before he left in the morning. His whole body hurt. With a groan, he sat up without opening his eyes. "Edgar?"

A hand pushed him back down. "Don't move, dumbass." That wasn't Edgar's voice.

"Zeke?"

"Yeah. I'm here even though you said you're not going to be my best friend anymore."

Amar opened his eyes. Light diffused into the room. He looked down to see bandages covering his arm and side. Memories returned. "You did this to me."

Zeke indicated his arm, which was in a cast and a sling, and his leg that was also in a cast. "You did this to me. We're even."

"We'll never be even. Edgar—"

"His flight arrived safely this morning, and Tito made sure a company car picked him up and took him home." Zeke pressed his lips together. "Amar, please listen to me."

"No."

Zeke closed his eyes, fighting a wave of pain. "You've been my best friend since we met at orientation our first day at Draco."

"My mistake." Amar tried to swing his legs out of bed, and that was when he noted the extent of his injuries. His entire left side was a mass of raw, ripped up skin. Being a shifter meant the majority of it would heal without scars, but it would take time to recover. Searing pain made his vision go black.

"Fuck—don't get up. I'm too banged up to keep putting you back in bed. Just listen to me."

Since he didn't have the strength to get far, Amar settled back into bed. Edgar was safe at home. All things considered, it was better for him to be there than to be here, where everyone Amar had once trusted had turned against him. Amar closed his eyes. Zeke could talk or not. He wasn't going to listen.

Zeke didn't seem to notice the hatred seething from Amar. "When Tito first proposed having you marry Anshu, I was against it. I mean, you should get to choose who you marry, right? But then I thought about it. Anshu is so much like you. He did a profile match thing, and it came out that you're almost a hundred percent compatible. So I didn't think it would hurt to meet him. I didn't think you were fucking your assistant. You said you weren't."

The last time he'd spoken on the topic with Zeke, he hadn't been. A lot had changed since Amar stopped pretending he didn't have deep and abiding feelings for Edgar.

"You've never been unreasonable before. I expected you would turn the idea down initially, but I thought you'd eventually come around. Anshu seems like a great guy, and he's an omega. You could

91

have kids. You've always wanted a family. You know how rare that is. We're an endangered species. Dragons are dying out because there aren't enough omegas to make breeding pairs. Anshu has his pick of the dragon world, and he chose you. That means you can have what you've always wanted."

"It sounds like you want him. Take him." He broke his silence with a vehement growl. "I want that with Edgar."

"You don't even know he's an omega, or if he's compatible with a dragon." Zeke sighed. "Grange, you're my best friend. I don't want to lose you over this. I thought I was doing what was best for you and for Draco."

"Let me guess—Tito convinced you this was the only reasonable course of action."

"I would jump at this chance," Zeke snapped. "But Anshu and I are not compatible."

Compatibility depended on more than desire. There were mystical and biological elements to consider. If Amar hadn't met Edgar, he would have been open to the idea. But even if it meant he'd never have offspring, he only wanted Edgar.

Zeke's gaze slid to the floor, and for the first time, he looked truly miserable. "I hate being at odds with you."

"I hate that you helped drive away the man I love and then incapacitated me so I couldn't go after him." Due to the damage to his side, he couldn't roll away from Zeke to dismiss him. Instead he closed his eyes.

Chapter 10

Edgar

Slivers of light showed through the dark slats in the barn, bringing with them frigid blasts of air. Edgar shivered and hugged his jacket closer around his body. He'd huddled in the farthest corner of the cage and burrowed into the remnants of hay left on the concrete floor, but it didn't seem to matter where the temperature was concerned.

He had no way of knowing exactly where he was, but he didn't think he'd left the Andes.

A week, give or take, had passed, and he'd been imprisoned in a cage too small to stand up or stretch out. The bars were too close together for him to shift into his smaller canine form and escape. He'd already tried. That left him at the mercy of his captors, the leader of which was Mr. Tito Kaysar, Amar's boss. For months, Edgar had listened to Amar talk about Kaysar as if he was the best person in the world. Mr. Kaysar was responsible for opening doors and providing the opportunities that helped Amar achieve a high level of success in a short amount of time.

Mr. Kaysar was a bad, bad man.

The wound in his head had ceased laying him low with headaches that made him want to tear out his eyes, but now he was worried something was wrong with his stomach. It fluttered and moved, like parasites were feasting in there. What was in the food they were feeding him that would cause these symptoms?

Wouldn't it be easier and more expedient just to kill him?

A door opened, and bright light blinded Edgar. He'd spent so much time in the dark, it was physically painful to be hit by that much light. He held up his hands as a shield until he made out Mr. Kaysar's form.

The large shifter squatted down for a closer look. "If I knew what kind of shifter you were, this would be a lot easier."

Edgar glared.

"If you haven't guessed, you're breeding. We weren't sure before, but we've tested your blood, and it's confirmed. Does your kind lay eggs or have live births?"

The glare melted into shock.

Tito didn't seem to notice. "We'll be moving you to a more secure facility, make sure you have proper nutrition and care, and then once you give birth—or lay the egg—you'll be considered for a pilot of our breeding program. If your offspring are viable, you'll be impregnated again. If not, you're of no use to us."

He moved back, and three large men came into the barn. The bars on one side slid up, and one man crawled in. Edgar cowered in a corner, but the man was stronger. He wrangled manacles onto Edgar's wrists and ankles, and then he dragged the weakened omega out.

Edgar found himself shoved into a smaller cage welded into the back of a dark van. It had air holes, but they were so small that Edgar couldn't see much through them. The ride lasted for a long time, and he was not given bathroom breaks. They arrived at their destination in the middle of the night. He was taken from the cage where he found himself stripped down. They turned a hose on him to wash away a week of not showering and being locked in a cage.

Then they herded him into a small room. It had a bed, a sink, and a toilet. He sank down on the mattress and put his head in his hands. Was Amar looking for him, or had he written off the loss of a lover and personal assistant because he was committed to wedded bliss with that giant blond man? It was hard to have hope because the only person he knew who would unquestionably search for him was Brielle, and she didn't stand a chance against these ruthless dragons.

Amar

Dragons, thankfully, recovered quickly from injury. Amar called Edgar regularly, but the phone went straight to voicemail. His omega was hurt, devastated by events neither of them could have predicted. This conversation would need to take place in person.

Waiting was pure hell.

A week later, Amar boarded a plane home. Zeke had tried to talk to him several times about everything, but Amar wanted nothing to do with him. As far as he was concerned, Zeke's betrayal was unforgivable. Eli and Koren had unsuccessfully attempted to reconcile as well. Tito had the sense not to step foot in the same room as Amar.

He went straight from the airport to Edgar's place. As the driver navigated to the address, Amar realized he'd never once taken his lover on a date. Their evening ski lesson had been the most romantic evening they'd spent—and it hadn't even been planned.

Amar had a lot to make up to Edgar if they were going to build a life together.

He stopped the car in front of the small house where Edgar lived with his sister. In the light of day, it still looked dilapidated, but he could see the small touches that showed an effort to make it look better. Squares of neatly clipped lawn lined a walkway that had been swept. Flower beds perched on either side of a concrete porch featuring pots that spilled over with blooms.

Amar opened the screen door and knocked on the scuffed up metal door. A chorus of dogs barked inside.

The door inched open, and a petite face painted with curiosity regarded him. "Can I help you?"

"I'm here for Edgar."

With a grin, she leaned down and grabbed a dog before opening the door wider. "Come in."

He hadn't expected a warm greeting. Honestly he hadn't expected to be let inside without a lot of begging, pleading, and apologizing.

The woman facing him was small, perhaps five feet tall. She was thin and pretty, with dark hair and eyes and skin. Edgar's sister was black.

He offered a hand. "I'm Amaricio Granger. You must be Brielle?"

"Yes. It's nice to meet you, Mr. Granger." She shook his hand, her grip strong and able. Her nose scrunched up. "Edgar isn't home yet."

"Where did he go?" Amar was willing to go anywhere, do anything to find Edgar.

"He went to Chile with you, and you guys stayed a few extra days." She laughed, a musical sound that invited him to join in.

If dread hadn't pooled in his stomach, he might have. "He left there five days ago. We had a misunderstanding."

Brielle went silent. She stared at Amar with wide eyes. "What kind of misunderstanding?"

"The bad kind." Amar ran a hand through his hair. "He hasn't called you or anything?"

She gazed at him, uncertain. "He said you'd be in the mountains, so I figured there was no cell service."

Amar closed his eyes. "Brielle, please—if he's angry and you're covering for him, that's fine. I understand. I just need to know he came home safely. I need to know he's okay."

She shook her head. "He didn't come home, and he hasn't called. I expected him home a few days ago, but when he didn't come home, I called your office. Kimbra said you'd extended your stay." She clapped her hands over her mouth. "Did something happen to him?" Her eyes darted around. "Did he do something weird?"

Amar clenched his jaw. This was the person who'd counseled Edgar to subvert his true self. "Like shift into a dog?"

Her eyes bulged, and she hugged the small dog in her arms closer to her. "Maybe he got quarantined at the airport?"

"No. My company said he got on the plane and that he was picked up and taken home." Amar closed his eyes. Zeke had relayed that information. What if he'd lied? In the whole course of their disagreement, he hadn't expected Zeke to lie. They didn't see eye-to-eye, and that was a problem, but he'd thought Zeke had told him the truth.

"Then where is Edgar?" Setting the dog on the floor, she wrung her hands together, and her eyebrows pinched in distress. "It's not like him to go off in a huff, not without telling me first."

"I don't know." He ran a hand through his hair, wracking his brain for an idea about where Edgar would have gone. It didn't take long for him to zero in on Tito. His mentor had to know where Edgar was. After all, he'd provided transportation to the airport. "I have to go. I need to find where Edgar could have gone."

Brielle jumped up. "I'll go with you."

Setting a hand on her shoulder, he stopped her. "This isn't going to be pleasant. You're a tiny thing, and I'll be dealing with big men who turn into even larger dragons. Edgar would kill me if I let anything happen to you."

After a moment of shock where she seemed to accept the idea dragon shifters existed, she shook off his hand and grabbed her purse. "I'll drive."

Edgar's relationship with Brielle made so much more sense. She definitely called the shots. She was small, but mighty. He didn't argue with her because if Edgar was still angry with him, then his best chance would be for Brielle to do the talking. He resolved to protect her because it's what Edgar would want him to do.

He directed her to Tito's house. The titular head of the Sharp-Winged Tribe had a ranch in a rural area about a couple hours outside of the city. High up in the mountains, it had the kind of inaccessible terrain dragons preferred.

As they approached, a car came up behind them. It moved quickly and without regard to the ravine below. Brielle's older model car didn't handle as well, and she lacked preternatural reflexes.

"Brielle, pull over."

The second car stopped behind them. Amar leaped out of the passenger side and marched to the unwanted intruder. "Zeke, I will kill you if you get in my way."

Zeke got out of the car and lifted his hands in the air. "I come in peace. Well, not peace. I did some digging, and I found out Edgar wasn't on the plane. They lied to me."

Amar regarded his former friend warily. He'd already arrived at the conclusion Edgar hadn't flown home. If he had, his first order of business would be to find Brielle. There was nobody Edgar loved and trusted more than his sister—not even Amar. Yet. "Why should I trust you?"

Zeke shrugged. "You have no reason. But I came here for the same reason you have—I want answers, and Tito isn't anywhere in the city."

Their caravan made it to Tito's place in a half hour. Nobody answered a knock at the door, and the ranch had an abandoned feel to it. Mountain peaks rose around them, mostly lined with trees. Around the house, they'd been cleared away. They didn't start again until after the old barn sitting a few acres away.

Next to them, Brielle stood with her hands on her hips, surveying the house and the valley below. "Can you pick up his scent?"

Zeke's head whipped around.

If it was fresh and strong, he could, but otherwise, he couldn't. Edgar's scent didn't seem to be around, but that didn't mean anything. Amar shook his head. "That's not one of my superpowers."

"It's one of Edgar's." Brielle rocked back on her heels. "I don't know what to do. I'm used to Edgar always finding his way back to me."

That was because she was his family, and he had a strong instinct to stay with his pack. Amar put his arm around Brielle's shoulders. "I'm not going to stop until I find him."

Zeke set a hand on Amar's wrist. "And I'll be right there with you."

Amar wasn't sure how he felt about that. Right now the only person he trusted unconditionally was Brielle, and that was because Edgar trusted her.

"Let's check the barn." Amar wasn't willing to throw in the towel so quickly. Perhaps Tito wasn't in the house, but that didn't mean he wasn't on the property. The absence of a car didn't mean anything because Tito could fly to his mountain retreat easier than he could drive there.

He motioned for Brielle to stay behind him and Zeke. He wasn't sure he should trust the man who'd been his friend for so many years, but he didn't see where he had a choice.

Midway across the field, a giant dragon landed in front of them. Fading sunlight absorbed into its dark scales, and steam exited from its nostrils.

Behind him, Brielle drew in a sharp breath.

Amar crossed his arms. "Where is Edgar?"

Faster than the blink of an eye, Tito morphed into his human form. In all his naked glory, he approached. "Amaricio Granger, I made you the man you are today. While I will take no pleasure in destroying you, rest assured I will do it anyway."

He knew his pursuit of a man of whom Tito didn't approve would create tension in their relationship, and Amar was prepared for that. However, his mentor's virulent threat took Amar by surprise. "What are you talking about?"

"Forget Edgar Vidal."

"Never." Not as long as he had breath in his body. "What have you done with him?"

Tito's expression darkened, and a menacing growl Amar had never before heard infused his voice. "I asked you for one favor—one thing that would save Draco International. You agreed, and then you reneged on your promise."

Amar's word was his bond. He wasn't in the habit of breaking it. "You tricked me." He puffed out his chest to show he wasn't afraid of the seasoned dragon leader. "If I had known you wanted me to marry an Ice-Breather, I never would have agreed."

"A few months ago, you would have." Tito jabbed a finger at Amar. "Before that fucking runt of an assistant came into your life, you would have agreed."

"Wait," Zeke said. "You're the one who suggested Amar hire an assistant. You wanted him to find someone."

Smoke streamed out of Tito's nose, evidence of his growing ire. "I had it all set up. Kimbra would have hired Anshu Bray if Amaricio hadn't circumvented the hiring process. I had her set it up in a way that would ensure the omega dragon got the job."

Kimbra knew about this? Her betrayal hit Amar like an iron fist in the gut. He closed his eyes to banish the distraction. He'd deal with Kimbra later. "Regardless, I love Edgar. Tell me where you've put him."

Brielle pushed between Amar and Zeke. Chest heaving with indignation and venom, she waved a warning finger in front of Tito's face. "Tell me what you've done with my brother, you naked old fart."

Before Tito could incinerate Brielle, Amar pushed her behind them. Then he stepped forward, stopping an inch from Tito's face. "Tell. Me. Where. Edgar. Is."

Tito laughed, a sound carrying such evil and hatred that Amar was knocked backward. "Listen here, you fucking useless piece of garbage: Edgar is safe—for now. If you do everything I tell you to do, then he will remain in that state."

The entirety of Amar's love for and devotion to Tito crumbled. He'd idolized a man who had no regard for him at all. If Amar wasn't so fucking worried about Edgar, he would have been crushed. As it was, his alpha nature rose to the fore. "If you harm one inch of him, I'll kill you slowly."

That evil laugh sounded again. This time, Tito followed it with a resounding punch to Amar's head. In the face of the unexpected blow, Amar spun and landed on the ground.

Brielle's hands fluttered over him as he got to his feet. He pushed her out of harm's way and faced Tito. Hatred boiled in his veins. "You're a fucking coward. You want to control me—my career, my apartment, my choice in mate. Well, you can't. I won't let you. I quit, you bastard."

"I quit also." Zeke moved between Amar and Tito, shoving himself in the way so Tito couldn't take another swing at Amar.

"No, you don't." Tito chuckled, a sound that chilled Amar to his bones. "Neither of you will be allowed to leave Draco International—ever. You belong to me. I found you. I trained you. I made you both the men you are today. You think you have morals or principles?" He threw his head back and let loose with a hearty laugh. "From the first day you began working here, you pledged your loyalty to Draco International—to me. Amar, you've hidden assets and massaged numbers to make them work out for us. Zeke, as the head of security, you've handled some delicate cases. If DI didn't back you on those—ahem—incidents, then you'd be in prison."

Amar had nothing to say. He had engaged in some questionable and creative accounting for the sake of DI. Tito had the capacity and the evidence to bury him.

Tito's dark eyes gleamed with malice. "Both of you will return to work. You will do your jobs. Ezekiel, you will continue to protect DI's interests, and you will continue to spy on the competition, stealing their ideas as warranted. Amaricio, you will salvage this project from the Ice-Breathers. I have smoothed over your appalling behavior from last week, and Anshu Bray is still willing to marry you. The date is set."

Amar's whole body rebelled. "I'm not fucking marrying anyone but Edgar. Where is he?" Fury made Amar's body tremble. His fingers morphed to talons, and his legs grew, bursting the seams in his pants.

Tito watched, unimpressed. "As long as you do what I say, he's safe. The minute you step out of line, he pays the price." Tito morphed back into dragon form. His voice sounded inside Amar's head. "You're welcome to stay and poke around, but you're wasting your time. He's not here. I've hidden him where you'll never find him. Don't be late for work. I'd hate to have to give the order to hurt your precious assistant. He's so small and delicate. I'm not sure how much he can take."

The terrible dragon took flight, and Amar sank to his knees.

Brielle tugged at his arm. "You have to go after him. You have to find Edgar."

If he went after Tito, he risked Edgar's life. He put a hand over Brielle's. "I can't."

She jerked it away and stalked in the direction of her car. "Fucking coward."

Zeke knelt next to Amar. "I don't know how, but we're going to find him and rescue him. And we're going to bring down Tito Kaysar. That's going to happen."

Numbly, Amar nodded. "I have to stop Brielle. If something happens to her, Edgar would never forgive me."

Chapter 11

Edgar

Being alone in a plain room for days on end made time seem not real. On one hand, hours might pass, and he wouldn't notice. Or he might be aware of every excruciating minute.

He had no idea what they planned to do with him. After mending his wounds, they'd locked him in a small room with white walls and no windows. It had basic furniture—a bed, a chair, a table, and a toilet with a sink in the top of the tank. Someone had stocked it with a few books and a crossword magazine. While it wasn't paradise, it was better than some of the foster homes into which he'd been placed.

Nobody beat him here. Nobody tried to molest him. In fact, outside of meal deliveries and daily medical checkups, they seemed oblivious to his existence.

With a sharp snick, the lock on the door disengaged. Edgar glanced up from his stimulating crossword for a brief second before deciding to ignore his visitor.

"Mr. Vidal, it's time for your ultrasound."

This travesty went on every day at ten in the morning. He knew this because the ultrasound room had a clock. With a sigh, he sat back in his chair. "Are we really doing this again?"

"Yes, Mr. Vidal."

He turned around slowly, nailing the burly technician with a stern glare. "You do know that men don't get pregnant, right? That's a woman thing."

"Yes, Mr. Vidal." The first week, the staff had argued with him when he made that claim. Now they ignored it.

He followed the technician down a hallway and past armed guards, stopping at a large room filled with medical equipment.

Edgar settled on the exam table, lifting his shirt and moving the waistband of his pants down. The first time they'd done this to him, he'd fought it. Eventually he realized they had no intention of raping him. They wanted to perform an ultrasound.

That's where the weirdness factor grew.

"Good morning, Mr. Vidal." Another tech, this one a woman, squirted jelly onto his stomach. "Let's see how those babies are doing."

She ran the paddle over Edgar's stomach.

Edgar watched the monitor, interested to see what horrible graphics they came up with today to try to convince him that he was pregnant. The artificial sound of heartbeats came through the machine as three small beans came into view.

"Oh, look at those babies. They're getting so big. It looks like you're coming into the next stage. Look." She put an arrow on the screen and pressed a button to take a picture. "See that? They're almost fully developed. That's a hand with one, two, three, four, five fingers. Let's get a count of all those fingers and toes."

She said more about growth and development while Edgar wondered what kind of fucked-up psychology experiment they had going on there. They were trying to make him feel good about something by engendering some kind of maternal instinct. Of course he looked at the screen. With the nothingness of his days, it was the only real entertainment he had available.

It was cruel as well. Edgar had never thought he'd get to have kids, but he knew Brielle would one day, and he'd be a very involved uncle.

With a snort, he lifted his gaze to the technician. "You people are bonkers."

"And you, Mr. Vidal, are going to be a father very soon—in about six weeks. It would be easier if you told us what kind of shifter you are, but since you won't, I'm estimating." She looked him over, her finger pressed to her lips as she thought. "Canine, perhaps. My research is pointing in that direction, and the timetable of fetal development matches."

Fear stabbed at Edgar's heart. He didn't know why it was imperative they not find out what kind of shifter he was, but he went with his instinct. These people did not have his best interests at heart.

"You stay in character really well."

She peered at him. "Mr. Vidal, if you stop for a moment to pay attention to your body, you'll find I'm not at all crazy. You're an omega shifter, which means if you have sex while you're in heat, you'll get pregnant."

Again, only female dogs went into heat. Edgar was a regular old horn-dog. He rolled his eyes.

The door opened, which was unexpected. All the other times, the guards waited until the tech cleaned the jelly from his stomach before entering.

Only this wasn't a guard. It was Tito Kaysar. He waved a small, folded piece of paper in the air. "Edgar, great news."

He handed the paper to Edgar, and Edgar realized it was an invitation printed on thick, cream-colored paper. Though he wanted to throw a punch at Kaysar, he refrained because two guards had followed the bad dragon into the room.

Edgar read the note to find it was an invitation—to Amaricio Granger's wedding with Anshu Bray. A fist squeezed Edgar's heart. All this time, he'd held onto a tiny string of hope that Amar would find him.

But if he thought objectively about it, he could admit Amar probably had moved on. After all, he'd only been with Edgar for one day. Sure, they'd grown close through the course of their daily interactions for the past few months, but what did that really mean? Edgar was replaceable, both as an assistant and as a lover.

He handed the invitation back to Kaysar. "I hope you don't expect me to send a gift."

Kaysar patted Edgar's stomach. "This is gift enough. Soon we'll know whether these offspring are viable. Dragon DNA is stronger than that of most other shifters, so we have every reason to believe you're carrying the next generation of the Sharp-Winged Tribe."

Edgar felt small flutters in his abdomen. He'd felt them before, but for the first time, he didn't discount them as gas. He rubbed his hand over his swollen abdomen and admitted it wasn't from too much rich food and a lack of exercise.

He was pregnant. Fucking pregnant.

He was having triplets—Amar's babies.

And Tito Kaysar had every intention of taking them away from him and impregnating him again.

No matter whether Amar had forgotten about him or not, he had to find a way out. He couldn't just stay here and let them use him like this. It was sick and wrong on so many levels.

Impulsively, he handed the invitation back.

Kaysar waved. "You keep it." He turned to leave, and Edgar leaped.

He landed on Kaysar's back, screaming and punching at the larger man's head.

Hands pulled him away, and a sharp jab on his thigh was the last sensation he felt before oblivion enveloped his mind.

Amar

"Kimbra, did Eli email those numbers I asked for?" Amar avoided meeting Kimbra's gaze. In the past month, he'd been working in secret to find where Tito might have stashed Edgar. It would have been nice to have Kimbra's help, but he didn't know where her loyalties lay, so he'd been going around her.

She sat across from him, watching him closely. Did that mean she was gathering intel to share with Kaysar, or was she worried about him? "Yes, Mr. Granger. They're in the shared folder."

He clicked through the levels to find the folder in question. The document, which had not been there moments ago, appeared. "There it is. Thanks. I need you to track down the receipts for the items I'm flagging."

Since he'd given her an assignment, he expected she would go to the outer office and complete it. Instead she set her tablet on the edge of his desk and sat up straighter. "Mr. Granger, I'd like to talk to you about Edgar."

"No." The topic of his missing lover wasn't open for discussion—especially not with someone he wasn't sure he could trust.

"Too bad." She rose and parked her hands on her hips. "Since he quit, you've been in a funk. I've tried to be understanding, but we've come to a point where I'm really concerned about you. Mr. Granger, it's not healthy. You're burning the candle at both ends, and your health is deteriorating. I'm heartsick at watching you work yourself to death. Why don't you just go talk to him?"

He lifted his gaze slowly. Was it possible she didn't know? Tito had claimed Kimbra was under his control, but was she really? He couldn't take the chance. "Close the door on your way out."

Kimbra huffed. "No. Amaricio Granger, you listen to me—you can't continue like this. I've tried to call Edgar, and he won't talk to me.

I went by his house, and his sister won't let me past the porch. Something is going on here, and I want to know what it is."

Her ire—and her concern—seemed so real. The barest twinges of hope thrummed in my chest. "Kimbra, when you set out to hire an assistant for me, did you have someone specific in mind?"

She frowned. "You mean like a friend I hoped to hire?"

"Perhaps." Might as well start there.

"No. None of my friends would put up with you." Her eyes widened as she realized what she'd said. "I didn't mean it like that. It's just that you're sometimes hard to handle. You can be very harsh, like now."

He had reason to be harsh. The man he loved had been kidnapped and was being used as leverage to keep him in line. He'd spent every waking moment looking for evidence that could lead him to where Tito might be holding Edgar—all the while hiding his trail.

Silently, he waited for Kimbra to continue.

She pursed her lips as she thought. "There was one thing."

He folded his hands and waited.

"Mr. Kaysar personally recommended someone. I don't remember who, but I have the note I made somewhere."

"Anshu Bray."

Her eyes lit. "Yes. That sounds right. You hired Edgar before I got too far into the first round of interviews."

Amar pushed a little more. "What was your impression of him?"

"I didn't have an impression because we never met." She made an impatient sound. "Mr. Granger, I'm trying to talk to you about Edgar, not some guy I didn't hire. What's going on? I went to Human Resources, and they won't give me answers. Something isn't right about all of this. I'm worried about Edgar and you. What happened in Chile?"

He wanted to take Kimbra into his confidence, but he didn't dare do it in his office because it might not be secure. "Pick up my dry cleaning and drop it by my place by six."

With that, he dismissed her. She must have understood the things he didn't say because she left without arguing.

The doorbell rang at a few minutes after six. Amar was relieved to find Kimbra there. She handed over his dry cleaning. "You need Edgar back."

He checked the hallway before closing and locking his door. "Tell me what you know."

Kimbra narrowed her eyes. "I told you what I know. You went to Chile with Edgar, and then I never saw him again. I can't get a straight answer from anyone about where he might be."

Amar gestured toward his sofa. "You'd better sit for this."

The story didn't take long to tell, and when he finished, he waited for Kimbra's reaction. It took a while to come.

"Wow." She whispered. "This is so much worse than I imagined. I thought maybe he confessed to being in love with you, and you were a jerk to him."

"Thanks," Amar said. "Your confidence in me is inspiring."

"Was that supposed to be a joke?"

He shrugged. Humor wasn't really his forte. He'd meant the comment sarcastically, but he couldn't seem to inject that much dryness into his voice. Mostly he was worried about Edgar.

"Mr. Granger, we have to find him."

"I know. Why do you think I've been working so hard?"

"Crunching numbers isn't going to help," she said. "You need gossip. Rumors."

"Numbers always tell a story. I think he's still in South America, but I'm not sure exactly where. I'm combing the data from there in the hope I stumble upon something that'll help me find him."

"What do you have so far?"

He scratched at his neck, a nervous habit that he'd kicked years ago. "I have a facility in the Andes owned by a proxy for Draco. It's used for atmospheric research, but somehow they have a ton of medical equipment."

"Okay," she said. "Why would you think Edgar is there?"

"I don't know. It's a feeling." He pushed his fingers through his hair. "I'm not someone who is comfortable operating on a gut feeling."

The ringing of the house phone interrupted their talk. Amar picked it up to find Zeke downstairs with Eli and Koren. He gave permission for them to come up.

Kimbra got to her feet. "Should I leave?"

"No. Pretend you're here because I'm still working."

She took a tablet from her bag and opened it up. "Yes, Mr. Granger. Let me look up those numbers for you."

He greeted Zeke, Eli, and Koren at the door. The trio came inside. As soon as the door was closed, Eli motioned for Amar to send Kimbra packing.

"She's discrete," Amar said. "Trustworthy."

Zeke sized up the fierce, diminutive assistant. "If you trust her?"

"I trust her."

"Okay," Eli said. "Tito got on a flight this morning. He went to Argentina."

It was a short jaunt from Argentina to Eli's villa in Chile. A look passed between them.

"I have his location," Kimbra said. "And I have his itinerary. There's a ten-hour hole in it where he's supposed to be visiting local landmarks."

Koren's eyes lit. "We need to find all Draco properties within six hours of his location in Argentina."

Amar didn't have to research anything. The facility his gut had chosen was well within those parameters.

Kimbra made the travel arrangements.

The snow-capped peaks of the Andes filled the view. He recalled a month ago, when Edgar had bounced in his seat and chattered excitedly about the incredible vista.

Now Amar just wanted to know which peak or valley hid his lover.

They left the airport in a rented car, and they drove to the Draco International atmospheric research facility. It was a small, squat building surrounded by high fences and barbed wire. Satellite dishes were on the roof, but nothing large enough to warrant a designation as a place that researched changes in the stratosphere.

Koren provided his R&D credentials to get them inside. They parked and went into the building. A guard sat behind a thick window just inside the entrance. "Papers, please."

Koren produced more papers. It seemed too easy. Amar became uneasy.

The guard studied them. "Doctor Tafari, welcome to Draco International's Chile branch. Who do you have with you today?"

"Research volunteers."

They weren't sure what was going on at the facility, but this seemed to be a likely cover story given the equipment and medical codes on the invoices.

The guard's lip curled. "Identification."

Eli, Zeke, and Amar provided false documentation that Eli had put together, and the guard buzzed them through.

They proceeded down a long hall. "Tito is likely getting a notification right now," Eli said. "We need to be quick and efficient."

Zeke stopped in front of a stylized site map under heavy plastic on the wall. "There's a sublevel." He tapped a point where it didn't look like there was anything.

"How do you know?" Amar studied the same schematic.

"I'm head of security for a reason," Zeke said. "Water and sewer hookups run way too deep for them to be for just a basement. I say we start there."

As Zeke whispered instructions, guards appeared at either end of the hall, training automatic rifles on each of them.

Zeke lifted his hands in the air. "Was it something I said?"

"You do not have authorization to be here," one of them replied. "You will be escorted from the property."

Having come this far wondering whether they were on a wild goose chase, Amar took this as validation. He shifted and breathed fire in one direction while Zeke took care of the opposite one.

In a hail of screams, the guards backed up, shooting bullets into the flames. The four of them shifted, their scales providing a sturdy armor.

Koren and Eli pulled them into the stairwell where they shifted back into human form because four huge dragons didn't fit on a single set of stairs.

Their clothes had shredded during the shift, leaving the quartet as naked as the day they were born. Losing no time, they descended the stairs on silent, bare feet.

Weaponless proved to be less of a problem without clothing. They emerged from the stairwell, shocking two guards into playing statue long enough for them to knock them out and take their weapons and access cards.

Through the access point, a corridor had locked rooms with narrow Plexiglas viewing windows. Each room was empty. Amar had a bad feeling about the whole thing, but he crept down the hall, peering inside each one until he found what he was looking for.

Wearing white pajamas, Edgar sat on a bed in a cramped room. He was curled in the farthest corner of the room with his head in his hands.

Amar tried opening the door, but it was locked. He slammed his hand against the glass. Edgar flinched, but he didn't look up. "Give me the fucking access card."

Koren hurried to him. He held up everything he'd taken from the guard—a badge, a gun, and a ring of keys. The lock was made for metal keys, so Koren tried one. Then another. And another.

Zeke pulled Amar back. "Let him work, Grange. If the key isn't there, we'll dismantle the door. Eli is looking for tools."

"Jackpot." Koren twisted a key and opened the door.

Amar rushed inside and fell to his knees. He wanted to pull his omega into his arms, but Edgar had yet to acknowledge his presence. "Edgar."

In lieu of a response, Edgar rocked back and forth.

Amar touched Edgar's hand. "Puppy—it's me. I came to take you home."

Edgar froze. He lifted his head, revealing a gaunt and haggard face. He stared at Amar, but no flash of recognition altered his blank expression.

"He's on heavy meds," Koren said. He stood in the door, flipping through a medical chart. "He probably thinks he's hallucinating." Koren lifted another paper. "He might also be hallucinating."

Edgar's hand inched forward, shaking with effort. It didn't stop until it came into contact with Amar's face. A melancholy ghost of a smile lifted the corners of Edgar's lips ever so slightly.

"He's pregnant."

Amar's head jerked, moving him away from Edgar's questing fingers. He fixed his stunned gaze on Koren whose eyes scanned the words on the page. "He's pregnant?"

"Yes. Congratulations. You're going to be the father of triplets." Koren's lips moved as he continued reading.

Zeke stuck his head in. "Is he okay?"

"No, he's not." Amar grasped Edgar's hand and brought it to his cheek. "I'm here, Edgar, and I'm taking you home. Brielle is going to be really happy to see you. Kimbra too."

A bit of the fog cleared from Edgars deep brown eyes. His gaze roved Amar's face, and a spark of recognition lit. "I like these drugs," he whispered. "Thank you for this."

A single tear tracked down his cheek.

Amar thought the heavy weight that had squeezed his heart for the past month would ease when he found Edgar, but it didn't. Seeing what he'd been through was like a hot poker being rammed into his gut over and over.

He grasped Edgar's face between his hands. "I'm here, puppy. For real. I'm taking you home, and I'm going to kill the bastard who did this to you."

Everything Tito had done for Amar crumbled under the weight of this betrayal. Now that he had Edgar back, Tito had nothing to hold over him. He was free. Well, soon they'd be free. Right now they needed to find a way out of the facility.

Edgar seemed to have a moment of lucidity, but it slid away too quickly to be sure.

Eli came in. He tossed a pile of folded clothes in his lap. "Put these on. We need to get him out of here."

Amar jammed his legs into the pants Eli provided. They were snug, but he only cared about getting Edgar out of there. He lifted Edgar in his arms, noting the swell of his omega's abdomen, and followed Eli down the hall. Koren and Zeke were already there, armed with weapons they took from the guards on the sublevel.

"Stay behind us."

Carrying Edgar meant Amar couldn't effectively fight. He followed Eli, Koren, and Zeke up the stairs. Armed men waited one floor up.

Zeke and Eli motioned for him and Koren to stay put. Against his better judgment, he allowed his friends to go ahead of them. Precious seconds passed. He moved to set Edgar down so he could fight with his friends, but Koren stayed him with a hand on his shoulder and a shake of his head.

"Wait for it," he whispered as he shoved a gun into the pocket in Amar's scrubs.

Zeke and Eli flew down the steps. "Get down."

An explosion rocked the building, and people screamed as the roof caved in on top of them. Eli, Zeke, and Koren shifted. Amar jumped on Zeke's back, and the three dragons took off through the hole in the roof, plowing through the debris.

Amar used his body to protect Edgar, who still wasn't aware of his surroundings. The omega slumped in his arms. He sighed, and his eyes fluttered closed.

Open sky surrounded them.

Chapter 12

Amar

Flying on their own power got them over the peaks of the mountains, all the way to Eli's villa in Chile. Flying on the back of a dragon wasn't easy. Amar much preferred to be the one in control; however he hated the idea of letting go of Edgar even more. His predator eyes kept a sharp watch for danger. It wouldn't take much for one of the dragon shifters at the facility to follow them. The journey took some time, more than three hours by Amar's estimation, and he didn't relax his guard for a second.

He'd already let others get the better of him once, and that had led to a month Amar would like to erase from existence. As they approached the mountain where Eli's villa was situated, patches of fog lent icy moisture to the chill air. Amar heightened his senses as much as he could without shifting. If he were in a position to attack an enemy, these made for optimal conditions.

The clear skies on the other side of the mountain had revealed no danger, and nothing happened on the foggy side either.

Finally, the trio of dragons touched down outside the vast house. Amar slid from Zeke's back with Edgar still in his arms. Eli, Koren, and Zeke shifted back to human form and went inside the house.

Edgar was more awake now, though he was still groggy from the sedatives he'd been given. He blinked his eyes open, and a new awareness spread through him. His body jerked. "Amar?"

"Yes, puppy. It's me. You're safe now."

He lifted his head and looked around. "Where are we?" His words were slow and blurred, though they were more distinct than before.

"We're at Eli's villa. It was the closest safe place for us to go. We'll rest up here, and then we'll go home."

"Home." Edgar's mouth trembled and the vibrancy in his eyes intensified. "Brielle."

"She's very worried about you. We all were. We'll call her as soon as we get you settled inside."

He wiggled to be set down, and Amar reluctantly released his hold on Edgar's legs. Keeping his arm around his omega, he helped his lover stand. Like a newly born fawn, Edgar's legs trembled as he found his footing.

"Don't know what they gave me," he said. "I attacked Mr. Kaysar when he told me you were getting married."

Amar wanted to be surprised about the supposed engagement, but he wasn't. Tito had shown him the same invitation, and he'd coupled it with a warning that if Amar didn't go through with it, then Edgar would pay the price.

"I'm not marrying anybody but you." Amar issued a firm assurance.

"Didn't think so." Edgar grinned. His pupils were wide with the effects of the sedative, but that was fading every second. "I knew you'd come for me."

Amar wondered what Tito had to gain from taunting Edgar like that. It was one thing to threaten Amar. He knew what Tito gained from having him under his control. But threatening and taunting Edgar made no sense. However, the man never did anything without a reason.

Zeke, Koren, and Eli emerged from the house fully clothed.

Koren scanned the sky, his eyes scrunched up to protect against the glare of the evening sun. "That was too easy."

Eli nodded sagely. "Agreed."

Though he agreed, Amar had a more pressing concern. He watched Edgar sway and stumble to the porch and sit down heavily on a step. "I'd like to know what they gave him and what the side effects are." Had they administered an addictive drug? It was completely outside Edgar's character to behave in a violent manner, even when provoked. He was the kindest, gentlest person Amar had ever met.

By way of response, Koren extracted a folded piece of paper from the pocket of Edgar's hospital scrubs. "I wasn't able to get the whole chart, but I got the most recent page. It has the name of the drug as well as pictures from the last ultrasound."

Edgar perked up. "The technician showed me the hands and feet." He hobbled over to them and peered at the paper that Koren scanned, and then he pointed. "There. That's a hand. See the fingers?"

Amar took the paper from Koren, taking his place next to Edgar. He studied the blurry, black-and-white image, his heart swelling as Edgar pointed out hands and feet, heads and hearts.

He still wanted to know about the sedatives Edgar had been given. Would they affect the babies as well?

"I wonder when you're due to give birth?"

Edgar shrugged. "The gestation period of the average canine is sixty-three days. Humans go for forty weeks. They could be ready to be born in a few weeks, or we may have to wait a few months. I'm wondering how they get out, and also where they're growing. I don't exactly have a uterus or a vagina."

"It's a mystical thing." Tito's voice came from behind the group.

Amar whirled, shoving Edgar behind him. Tito was alone, and he was naked, which meant that he'd flown in the same way they had. He must have landed a little ways away because they had neither seen nor heard his approach.

Tito spread his hands wide. "Omega shifters have an internal birthing chamber, much like mammalian females do, and that's where offspring gestate. When the babies are ready, a birth canal will form. Since you're a canine—for fuck's sake, Amar, you've impregnated a fucking *dog*—it'll be sooner rather than later."

Rage, the likes of which Amar had never felt, welled up inside. When Tito had been holding Edgar, fear and anxiety had pushed away the anger, and now, compounded by the emotions that had kept it contained, it exploded. Amar flew at Tito, his hand morphing to a talon as he ran, and he slashed downward.

Tito countered by morphing his skin to scales, a feat Amar had not yet mastered. To be fair, he hadn't spent much time practicing.

Amar's powerful claws scratched Tito's obsidian scales, but the blow didn't inflict much damage.

Arching one eyebrow, Tito regarded Amar. "Are you sure you want to fight me? I taught you everything you know, but I have not taught you everything I know."

Though Amar was a proficient fighter, his heart was made of equations and spreadsheets. He'd never put the time and effort into learning to battle that Tito had advised. Still, he had one thing going for him—a tornado of fury fueled him, more than enough to compensate for his lack. Amar had no doubt he would avenge his omega on this day.

Amar shifted his talon back into a hand, and he tried to breathe through the rage blinding him to reason. He wanted to tear Tito's limbs from his body. He wanted to tie him down, cut him open, and rip out his entrails. A slow death like that was no more than Tito deserved.

"It's good to see you've retained some sense." Tito laughed. "Amaricio, I know you're upset right now, but you have to understand I did this for us—for dragons. Birth rates have fallen off in the last few decades. You are among the last handful of young ones left, and if we don't figure out what's going wrong, then we're doomed."

It seemed to Amar that he had been able to impregnate Edgar just fine. Perhaps dragon shifters needed an infusion of fresh blood. There was too much inbreeding to keep them going in these disparate tribes.

These thoughts winged through the analytical part of his brain, but the animal part took over. The gun Koren had put into his pocket weighed heavily. Dragons weren't given to using weapons against one another, but right now Amar didn't care. He lifted his hand and pointed the gun straight at Tito. Before his former mentor could breathe a disparaging word, Amar pulled the trigger.

By the time the report finished echoing through the valley, most of them had overcome their shock.

Tito brushed imaginary dust from his arm. "You missed."

"On purpose," Amar said. "I'm not a murderer. I'll never be like you."

Edgar's arms wrapped around his waist. Koren took the gun from Amar's hand. "I know just the place for you, Tito."

Tito lifted his eyebrows. "You think you've won?"

"Did you bring backup, or were you hoping to blackmail us into compliance?" Zeke asked.

The answer was obvious—nobody had followed Tito.

"Where are you taking him?" Amar asked.

"I'm a researcher with questionable ethics," Koren said. "I have secret underground facilities all over the place. I even have ones Tito doesn't know about."

Amar tightened his hold on Edgar. "As long as he's in a place where he can't harm anyone, then I'm okay with it."

Edgar

The world still seemed somewhat ethereal, like he was watching a movie after having too many mimosas with Brielle. The gun's report eradicated the last of the malaise, bringing everything into sharp focus. He tightened his embrace, making sure Amar stayed grounded.

His boss wasn't the kind of man who went around hurting people. He was stern and efficient, an excellent leader, but he wasn't a murderer.

More than that, he could feel Amar's pain. So many different kinds crushed him, but in the midst of all that was an altruism, a goodness that couldn't be denied.

Edgar had overheard talk at that place, and he knew they hadn't considered cross-breeding shifters.

"Amar?" He reached up and stroked a caress along Amar's cheek. "Honey?"

The hateful look in Amar's eyes faded. "He won't bother us anymore."

Mr. Lowry—Zeke—bound Mr. Kaysar's hands and feet. "If you shift, this will dig in and cut off your limbs."

"Seems fitting," Mr. Tafari—Koren—said. "Actions have consequences, and all that."

Eli, Zeke, and Koren set to work transporting Mr. Kaysar to his new home while Amar escorted Edgar inside.

Amar was silent all the way to the room they'd shared before. Once they were alone, he dropped to his knees and pressed his cheek to Edgar's swollen abdomen. Edgar stroked his fingers through Amaricio's thick, dark hair.

"This, right here, is everything I hold dear. I don't know what stroke of fate or luck brought you to me that day, and you've come to mean the world to me, Edgar Vidal. I love you."

Edgar didn't know when he'd fallen in love with Amaricio Granger, only that he had. At first, he'd been afraid of messing up his job and even of the passion between them not lasting. But being locked away had given Edgar plenty of time to think. He'd been dealt a harsh hand in his life. As much as he'd tried to not let it get the better of him, he'd shied away from emotional entanglements because so many people had let him down so often.

He'd vowed that if he ever got out of that place, he was going to take a chance at embracing love and happiness.

"I love you too, Amaricio Granger."

Amar looked up at him, a fierce expression on his face. "Marry me."

"I thought you'd never ask."

Moving so quickly that his image blurred, Amar got to his feet and lifted Edgar in his arms. He claimed his omega with a deep, satisfying kiss.

Epilogue—Edgar

Working as a personal assistant for one's husband was an altogether different experience than working for a man about whom one merely had impure thoughts and fantasies.

Edgar stood behind Amar's desk in his home office and set out name cards for the guests they expected later that day. He set one hand on his huge abdomen, a habit he'd developed as it grew ever larger. "I thought we'd put Zeke next to the young man Brielle is bringing. She said he volunteers at an animal shelter and that he's super hot. And gay."

Seated in the chair next to Edgar, Amar squeezed Edgar's ass before pulling him onto his lap. "Zeke likes to sit next to Eli or Koren so they can talk about work." He followed up by pressing his lips to the curve of Edgar's neck.

Edgar sighed with pleasure, and his hand came up to cup Amar's cheek. "That's another great reason for breaking them up. All they talk about is work. That's boring. They need to meet people so they can broaden their horizons, and they need to flirt. Goodness—how they need to flirt. It's a valuable life skill that seems to have passed you all by. Otherwise they'll end up as stodgy workaholics who have no lives and no appeal to anyone."

Amar's hand slid from Edgar's knee and up his thigh. "Like me, before I met you."

In the past month since Edgar had returned and moved in with Amar, he'd managed to fit lots of fun things into Amar's schedule. In addition to walks or jogs through the park, they had romantic picnics and attended fun events around the city. There was too much to see and do, and Edgar wasn't one to resist the lure of a sunny day and the chance to get outside. He dragged Amar along, and he found his new husband smiling much more often.

Edgar giggled as Amar's hand cupped his cock. "Mr. Granger, I think we were in the middle of a work thing."

"Mr. Granger," Amar returned, "it's time for a break."

Before Edgar could comment, Amar scooped him up and carried him down the hall to their bedroom. His lips captured Edgar's in a searing kiss, and his hands wandered over Edgar's body, ridding him of clothing.

By the time Amar broke the kiss, they were both breathing hard, though only Edgar was naked. Amar eased Edgar onto the bed and kissed his way down the omega's body. Sensations, warm and titillating, fired through Edgar's synapses. By the time Amar's long, forked tongue licked away a drop of precum from Edgar's cock, Edgar was close.

Amar sucked that throbbing cock deep into his mouth, moans vibrating in the back of his throat to drive Edgar insane. The warmth of the foreplay became an inferno wending through Edgar's body. With a husky cry, he came. Amar's soft moans took on an urgency as he drank down Edgar's essence.

With spasms of orgasm still radiating through his limbs, Edgar drew his knees up and relaxed. Amar's lubricated cock sank into Edgar's rectum, connecting them in a way that always left Edgar breathless. He whimpered in ecstasy as Amar claimed him. The pair rocked together. Amar thrust faster, though he was careful to be gentle. The feel of his alpha inside completed Edgar. He felt fulfilled and whole, and he caressed Amar's strong shoulders. His forays extended down Amar's sexy chest, and he reached between them to stroke his cock that was already stirring.

"You're insatiable," Amar grunted.

"Where you're concerned—yes." Edgar pumped his hand along his shaft, enjoying the feel of being stimulated in two places. His cock lengthened. "I'm making more dessert for you, my darling."

Batting his hand away, Amar took over. He pumped his cock into Edgar to the same rhythm he used to stroke Edgar's dick. In moments, Amar's body stiffened as he orgasmed. Hot jets of semen bathed his insides, and Edgar luxuriated in the sensation.

Amar collapsed to the side, careful not to crush his pregnant husband. "Give me a minute. I'm going to do things to you, Edgar."

Laughter bubbled from Edgar, but the noise was interrupted by a sudden gasp. It felt like iron bands were squeezing his midsection.

Immediately Amar sat up. "What's wrong?"

"I think the babies are coming." He felt for Amar's hand, and he squeezed hard to help him through the contraction.

When it subsided, Amar jumped up and slid into his pants. "I guess that settles the question of who sits next to whom at dinner."

"Call Brielle," Edgar said. "She wants to be here for this."

Though the idea of omegas giving birth had been explained to Edgar several times, he didn't have faith that this magical birthing canal would form. In the past few weeks, he and Amar had taken classes in how to deal with the birth. They'd chosen to do it online because hospitals tended to think men giving birth was cause for scientific study. Edgar had enough of being studied.

"There isn't time." Amar gentled his tone as he lifted Edgar. "Let's get the blanket on the bed."

They had a soft waterproof mat to put over the bed to protect it from the fluids that accompanied a birth. Edgar waited for Amar to spread it out. "Are you sure you want to see this part? It's going to be gross."

Amar guided him to lay on the bed. "Shush, you. It's beautiful and wondrous. This is the arrival of our children."

"At least text Brielle. She can help once they're born."

With an exaggerated sigh, Amar gave in. "I'll be right back."

While he was gone, another contraction came. Edgar breathed through them the way he'd seen women do on television. Amar returned as Edgar groaned for the tenth time.

"Damn it, Edgar. This is why I didn't want to leave you."

The pain subsided, and Edgar grinned. "You need to let your parents know. They're super excited."

Amar's phone chirped. "Brielle is on her way, and I'll take care of notifying everyone later, when it's over. Right now, you're my priority. I'm not leaving your side again for anything."

"What about ice chips? I hear those are helpful to keep me hydrated."

"You're not going to need them."

Just then a contraction the likes of which the first two had not prepared him for gripped Edgar. He shouted in surprise and pain, grabbing for Amar's hand. "What the fuck is going on? Is it supposed to hurt that much?"

"I think so." Amar dabbed a towel at the sweat on Edgar's forehead. "Breathe through it."

Though sound advice, right now it rubbed Edgar the wrong way. "You fucking breathe through it. I want drugs. I want an epidural."

Amar settled on the bed next to Edgar and pulled him closer to snuggle. "It won't work."

Tingles in his nether regions warned Edgar that something magical was going on. "My hard-on is gone, and it feels funny under my balls."

"Spread your legs." Amar repositioned himself between Edgar's legs. A smile split his face. "Lift your knees. There you go. I see a head."

It seemed really freaking fast, but Edgar reasoned that the whole experience was magical on many levels.

He felt Amar's hands lifting his balls out of the way. "When the next contraction comes, push."

Edgar did what his alpha said, and the next thing he knew, he felt a whoosh between his legs.

"There's one." Amar lifted a small bundle. It was tiny, really, not much larger than puppy. He set it on Edgar's bare chest. The baby was small, about ten inches long, and it was perfectly formed.

Instinct had him putting his mouth over the baby's nose to suck out the goo. The hairless baby coughed and cried, flapping his tiny arms and legs. It was a boy. His face reddened with temper, which meant he took after Amar.

Worry stabbed through Edgar's heart. What if something was wrong with them? The doctor he'd been to hadn't known much about canine physiology. "I thought babies were bigger."

"You're a small dog, and baby dragons are extremely tiny. Don't worry—they'll grow."

Edgar glanced up from ministering to the baby. His gaze met Amar's and tenderness passed between them. A sheen of tears distorted Edgar's vision. "He's perfect, Amar—so very perfect."

Another contraction hit, and Amar stroked Edgar's thigh. "It's okay. Push if you need to. I don't see a head. Oh—there it is. Welcome, little one." As Edgar had done with the first one, Amar cleared the airways of this one, and then he handed the baby over to Edgar.

The second baby was a boy, and the third was a perfectly pink little girl. It happened quickly, and Edgar didn't know what to do first. Small but strong cries filled the air. He tried to soothe them, but his body wasn't done having contractions.

Amar took them away, one at a time, to bathe them with warm cloths. He wrapped each one in a blanket and returned them to Edgar.

"I should get a shower," Edgar said. The pad under him soaked up most of the bodily fluids. "When are the contractions going to stop?"

"Afterbirth." Amar got into position. "I almost forgot." He massaged the hard shell that was Edgar's abdomen. Another contraction tightened things up there. "Push. You can do this. We're almost there."

An hour later, Edgar and Amar bottle-fed two of babies, and Brielle took care of the third. Though Edgar was tired, joy suffused his heart. A month ago, he'd despaired of ever seeing sunlight again. Today he had a wonderful husband and three incredible pups.

He looked at Amar to find a smile splitting his husband's face as he fed the little girl.

Edgar's insides turned to mush, not that they'd been too solid since he set eyes on their bundles of joy. "I've never been so happy in my whole life."

"I never thought this level of joy was possible." Amar leaned over and brushed a kiss across Edgar's lips. "Thank you, my love."

"You're welcome." He beamed, and he deepened the kiss.

About A. J. Stone

A.J. Stone loves rainbows and bears. Visit https://michelezurloauthor.com/a-j-stone/ for the latest information or follow on Facebook at https://www.facebook.com/AJStoneBearsCove/ to keep up with the newest releases, and feel free to request stories for your favorite Bear's Cove characters.

Reviews let A.J. know you want more!

Bear's Cove Series (MM/MPreg) by A. J. Stone

Dak's Omega
Tanzil's Second Chance
Perfect Blend: Kofi's Omega

Draco International Series (MM/MPreg) by A. J. Stone

Amaricio's Omega Shifter
Koren's Omega Neighbor
Zeke's Reluctant Omega

MM Romance by Nicoline Tiernan

Nexus #1: Tristan's Lover by Nicoline Tiernan
Nexus #2: The Man of His Dreams by Nicoline Tiernan

Sneak Peek

Koren's Omega Neighbor (Draco International 2)

Chapter 1—Chay

Running under the cover of night was strangely exhilarating. Nobody was around, and Chay had the park to himself. His clothes were stowed in a small backpack hidden in a cluster of bushes that retained the faint odor of marijuana. The teens who'd been camped out there were long gone.

He spent some time sniffing, getting to know the lay of the land and the marking of various territories. Tonight was his tenth night sneaking out for a 4 am run, and he was feeling a little reckless, so he veered out of the park to explore the city streets. When the first streaks of light appeared on the distant horizon, he headed back to the park, shifted, and hurriedly dressed.

Then he jogged back to the high-rise in the expensive part of town where Great-Uncle Chayton was making him live for the next 172 days. The doorman, a woman, opened the door and nodded to him. "Good morning, Mr. Sadler."

"Morning, Courtney."

A different doorman had been on duty when he'd left. This was another advantage of his early morning jog—it coincided with shift change. Nobody could definitively track his comings and goings.

"Chayton Sadler V."

Chay stood in the lobby of the upscale apartment building. Someone saying his name drew his attention toward the row of mailboxes accessible by a tiny key he had yet to find.

The person in question had broad shoulders that were almost swallowed up by a mane of shaggy hair. His strong physique tapered to trim hips that had Chay looking closer. Long legs, long torso—this man was seriously tall. At six feet, Chay was not a small man, but next to this guy, he felt downright tiny.

Though the guy wore a wrinkled dress shirt with jeans, he didn't seem as out of place as Chay felt in the elegant main floor of his uncle's building.

"It's 'the fifth,'" Chay supplied. "Not 'V.'"

At the sound of his voice, the man turned. Clear, blue eyes regarded Chay with an intense sense of bafflement. "You're Chayton Sadler the Fifth?"

"Yeah. That's me." Chay had been in the building for a week, and he'd met a few neighbors. Most were professionals who were too wrapped up in their work to appreciate the luxurious amenities this place had to offer.

The bonus features didn't make up for not being at home with his pack, though. No hot tub, swimming pool, fitness room, tennis court, or restaurant could replace easy access to his fathers and siblings.

But the power of this mystery man's penetrating perusal made him forget to be homesick for the moment.

The man held up a stack of envelopes, but his gaze devoured Chayton's body. "You don't live in 14A."

Confusion made Chay slow to respond. Or maybe he should be outraged? Sure, he didn't dress in tailored suits, but neither did this hunk of gorgeous man. "It was my uncle's place. He passed away last month, and I inherited it."

The man's lips pressed together, but he appeared puzzled, not angry. "I live in 14A, and a female couple lives in 14B." He hooked his thumb through a belt loop, drawing attention to his loose-fitting jeans. One well-placed tug, and they'd probably slide right off. "What floor are you on?"

Chay frowned. "Fourteen. The elevator guy always takes me to fourteen."

Each floor held two apartments, neatly labeled A or B.

The guy held out the stack of mail. "You live in 13A, directly below me. The addresses here are off by one floor because the ground floor is called 'Main' and the second floor is called 'one'. Someone who didn't understand how numbers work made up the addresses."

Chay reached for the stack, and his hand brushed the handsome neighbor's mighty paw. A charge ran through him, and the dog part of him let loose with a subsonic whine.

The man stilled. That knowing gaze probed the depth of Chay's eyes for something. Time seemed to stand still with that handsome face frozen in a frown. Chay had the opportunity to note the light brown stubble staining the man's tanned skin and the tiny laugh lines around those entirely kissable lips. He wondered what it would be like to run his fingers through that mop of hair and what it would feel like for that stubble to scratch across his stomach.

This guy had to be almost twice his age. He was closer to Chay's fathers' ages than Chay's, but right now, Chay couldn't seem to care.

The years melted away, and his canine let loose another subsonic whine.

Releasing his hold on the mail, the guy took a step closer, his nose twitching as he—was he *sniffing* Chay? This dude was a canine shifter? Given his size, he had to be a Great Dane or an extra-large Pyrenees.

Chay squared his shoulders and straightened his posture. He kept his gaze glued to his upstairs neighbor. When the guy took another step closer, Chay backed up. "I didn't catch your name."

A rumbling came from deep in the man's throat. Was he purring? Maybe he was a cat shifter, maybe a panther or lion. Fuck—that meant he was dangerous. But he didn't seem like he was unstable. "Koren Tafari."

Tafari rhymed with safari, so maybe Koren was a lion shifter. Lions were known for being unpredictable, territorial, and they had violent tempers. Or he was way off. Maybe this guy was just strange.

Even if he was a shifter, Koren's intensity meant he was focused and possibly an apex predator. As a member of an easygoing breed, Chay could do without that kind of stress in his life. No matter how much his canine wanted to inhale Koren's delicious scent or rub his head against the man's side, he wasn't going to do it.

Chay stuck out a hand. "Hi, Koren. I'm Chay. It's nice to meet you. I'll get down to the post office first thing and get the address corrected. I'm sorry about the inconvenience."

Those blue eyes moved over his body, heat lasering away Chay's clothes and leaving no doubt as to the content of the older man's thoughts. "It's not an inconvenience. You're new to the city?"

The deep timbre of his voice rumbled through Chay's body, leaving a yearning shiver in its wake.

"Yeah. I grew up about twelve hours away." He meant to glance around the elegant lobby, but he found it impossible to break the hold Koren had over him. "I'm still figuring out where things are."

"You're a jogger?" Somehow, Koren managed to move closer, and Chay was just now noticing. He fingered the strap of Chay's backpack. "How far are you planning to go?"

By Chay's calculations, he'd covered at least a dozen miles. "I went already. I got a couple hours in."

Koren's brows lifted. "A serious runner sweats."

Dogs panted, and Chay had barely broken a sweat in the mile between the park and the apartment. Meeting Koren's challenge, he chuckled. "Do they?"

Again, Koren's gaze moved over him. "What kind of shifter are you?"

Oh—so they were going to get it all out in the open now?

Chay didn't blink. "Lab."

Koren grinned, a careless, flirty expression with a hint of lust. "I've always had an affinity for larger breeds."

"What are you?" He hoped Koren wasn't a tiger or anything that might eat a dog.

"Dragon."

Lots of creatures shifted, but to Chayton's recollection, they were actual animals that existed as non-shifters. Dragons were fiction. Backing up, Chay held up a hand. "Like a Komodo dragon?"

"Sharp-Winged."

"There's no such thing as—"

"There he is!" A squeal had Chayton breaking off mid-denial.

He and Koren both turned to regard the interloper with no small degree of annoyance. The short, round woman didn't seem to notice.

Her eyes sparkled with joy, and she stuck out her hand. "You must be the new guy in 13A. I'm Lizz—two z's—Buika. I'm in 1B. I'm president of the advisory and welcoming committees."

"Hi, Lizz with two z's. I'm Chay Sadler. It's great to meet you." Chay shook her hand. Nothing about her seemed supernatural, so Chay figured that, like most people he'd met, she wasn't a shifter.

"Chay Sadler?" Frowning, she gazed in confusion. "Chayton Sadler passed away last month."

"He was my great uncle. I was named for him. He's Chayton Sadler the Second, and I'm the Fifth."

Her mouth opened the slightest bit, a rainbow trout suddenly finding itself lifted out of water. "The fifth? What happened to three and four?"

"My dad is four, and his cousin is three. When I have kids, I'll do a sixth, just to keep the name going. I'll call him Cha-cha."

She giggled and waved her free hand. "Oh, you. So handsome. I see you've already met our resident mad scientist. Koren, are you just getting in?"

The smolder in Koren's gaze cooled considerably, but he still greeted Lizz warmly. "I was working."

Grabbing his arm, she clucked in disapproval. "You need to get out more. You'll be single forever if you spend your life locked in a lab."

At the utterance, the mischievous slant returned to Koren's smile. "Locked in a Lab. That sounds like fun."

Catching the innuendo, Chay choked on his saliva.

Koren slapped him on the back a few times, but mostly he rubbed circles that sent Chay's libido into overdrive. "You okay?"

"Fine," Chay said.

Even though he'd just been coughing into them, Lizz took both of his hands in hers. "Chay, I want to throw a welcome party to introduce you to the building. How about this Friday night at your place?"

Normally when a person threw a party for someone, they provided the venue. Chay wasn't quite certain how to react. For some reason, he glanced at Koren. "At my place?"

Koren pursed his lips. "It's so everyone can gawk at your stuff."

"Did you do this when you moved in?"

"I did," Lizz said. "I don't mind having the party at my place, but yours is so much bigger."

Chay couldn't quite think of a reason to refuse. "It's my uncle's stuff." He'd cleaned out some things, but there was still a lot left to go through.

"Even better." A smirk played around Koren's mouth. "Your uncle didn't socialize with anyone in the building."

No one in the building seemed to be all that social. So far, Lizz was the lone butterfly.

Chay's mind couldn't keep away from thoughts Koren. The man was a supernova—hot to the core. Dragons breathed fire. Maybe his core was made of the stuff. It would explain the intensity and the heat rolling from him and battering Chay on a cellular level.

Chay thought about what Basil would advise him to do. "How about Saturday night? That'll give me a little more time to get settled."

"Wonderful," Lizz clapped. "I'll deliver flyers to all the apartments. Koren, you're coming, right?"

He shrugged. "If I get back in time. I have a business trip planned." Then that molten gaze captured Chay's again. "Perhaps I can take you to lunch today?"

This was crunch time. If he refused, he was telling the shifter that he had zero interest in him. If he went, then Chay would need to figure out what kind of interest he really had in this man who claimed to be a dragon shifter. Were they drawn together because they were two shifters adrift in a sea of humans? Was Koren after a quick hook-up?

Chay didn't do quick hook-ups. He wasn't a hound dog. His breed was steadfastly loyal. He inhaled a huge breath. Lunch didn't mean sex, though it could mean flirting with this handsome neighbor. He grinned. "Sure. Why not?"

Lizz whipped out her phone. "Let's exchange numbers so we can work out details."

Koren backed away. "I need to get a couple hours of sleep. I'll knock on your door at one."

When he disappeared down the hall where the elevators were located, Lizz sighed. "You are so lucky, Chay. That man is seriously dreamy. I have a thing for nerds."

Koren didn't seem like a nerd. He had an athletic build and bearing, as did most shifters.

"It's just lunch," he said. "Koren was being nice." Where he was from, the entire neighborhood got together for a party whenever anybody new came in from out of town, even for a visit. New neighbors were a rarity, and they were always welcomed with open arms.

Lizz shook her head. "Koren Tafari is not a nice guy." Then her eyes grew wide. "I don't mean that he's mean or evil or anything, just that he avoids anything involving the welcoming committee or events we have so people in the building can get to know each other. It's not like he needs to network, not with his position as head of research and design at Draco International. He has plenty of friends."

She slapped her hand over her mouth.

"I talk too much," she mumbled behind her hand. "Gossip is my kryptonite. I gotta stop."

It was refreshing to meet someone who lacked artifice. Chay laughed, and Lizz's face reddened.